ONE HUNDRED WAYS

AN ASPEN COVE SMALL TOWN ROMANCE

KELLY COLLINS

BOOK NOOK PRESS

To every girl who felt she wasn't enough. You are.

CHAPTER ONE

Riley Black entered Aspen Cove on a wing and a prayer. She had four dollars and thirty-seven cents in her purse, and nothing in her bank account. Her old, beat-up Jeep limped into town on the fumes of her last fill-up a hundred miles ago. If she blinked once, she'd miss the entire town.

Pulling into an open space several spots down from Maisey's Diner, she thought twice about killing the engine. There was a good chance it would never start again if she did.

Her hand gripped the key as she took a steadying breath. One turn, and the old SUV shook and shuddered before it sighed into silence. In reality, it didn't matter if the engine never turned over again. She'd made it.

Her step-mom, Kathy, had told her she was running from her past, but Riley knew she was running toward her future. A future no one supported but her Aunt Maisey and her cousin Dalton. A future where she could finally be who she wanted to be, not who everyone told her she should be.

There were three things she knew for certain. First, she was an artist down to the scrap metal and welder's flame that surely ran through her DNA. Second, she couldn't live up to people's expectations, so she was content to live without them. Third, Aspen Cove had promised her a new beginning, a life where she could choose everything.

Her father's death several months ago had rocked everyone's existence. It was such a bizarre and unexpected accident. How did a man drown in a sink full of dishes?

Riley knew how it could happen. After a liter of vodka, a person could drown in their own spit. She'd kept her father's secret for years. He'd been running away too but only got as far as the bottles of booze he hid around the house could take him.

She never told her stepmother. The woman wouldn't have believed her if she'd tried. If Kathy Black hadn't been aware of her husband's drinking problem after close to three decades of marriage, there was no way to convince her now. Maybe she'd been aware all along and didn't want to admit her perfect life wasn't perfect after all. She had no problem pointing out others' imperfections but never saw her own.

Riley wanted more for herself but would never get it living near Kathy, who constantly told her she deserved less. If it weren't for her father, she would have been gone years ago.

She opened her door and stepped onto the asphalt. The cool fall air floated over her skin. It gathered in her broomstick skirt, sending the fabric rippling against her legs. The scent of pine and fresh mountain air wrapped around her, like a cozy blanket.

She'd always felt one with nature. Maybe that was why her nickname Granola Girl in high school never bothered her. She was a clean-eating, animal-loving, hemp-wearing modern hippie and proud of it. Or at least she would be now because, at twenty-seven, she would finally be able to be herself.

The car door screeched as she shut it. Probably nothing a can of WD-40 couldn't take care of, but that was a luxury she couldn't afford.

She glanced at her supplies in the back seat and wondered if her priorities might be skewed. She'd buy sheet metal, tungsten, and rods before she bought anything else. How telling was it that the space in her car was taken over by scrap metal, gloves, masks, and two welders? Her personal items filled a single suitcase and a milk crate.

She stretched her arms and rolled her neck, loosening the kinks from her long drive. Once her vertebrae had popped into place, she started toward the diner entrance. She couldn't wait to get inside and give her aunt a hug.

It was her Aunt Maisey who'd started her love of art. She'd bought her and her twin brother, Baxter, an erector set when they turned seven. The first sculpture Riley created was with that set. To make sure no one took it apart, Riley borrowed her father's soldering iron and fused it together. She got the spanking of a lifetime that day. Twice as many swats as necessary because she'd not only destroyed something that was only half hers and used the soldering gun without permission, something she wasn't allowed to touch, but she'd caught the kitchen on fire when she left it plugged in. It had burned a nice-sized crater in the table before Kathy's loan paperwork caught fire. That spread to the nail polish and remover that sat in the center of the table like condiments. Riley still had that fused erector set. Brought it with her to remind her safety came first, and dreams could come true.

The bell above the door rang when she entered. The smell of French fries filled her nose.

Every head in the diner turned her way. All three of them anyway. An old man sat in the corner, reading his newspaper. A woman at the window ate cherry pie, and a man with eyes that could steal a soul sat in a side booth. Why his eyes caught her attention, she couldn't say, but maybe it was because his irises were tinted with at least three different greens. She had an eye for color, the patina of his eyes moved from rich hunter green to moss green and finished at a laurel green.

"Riley," Aunt Maisey called from the pass-through kitchen window. "Is that you?" Her straw-yellow bouffant bobbed in every direction as she raced through the swinging doors and headed toward Riley like a runaway train.

Maisey's white loafers squeaked to a halt in front of her before wrestler-strength arms pulled her in for a big hug.

"Oh, my God." Maisey walked around her like a buyer looking at a heifer at the 4H fair. "You've grown."

Riley laughed. "It's been a long time." Ten years was way too long to keep family apart.

4

Maisey shook her head. "How's Kathy holding up?"

It struck her as odd that Maisey would inquire about her stepmother, given it was Kathy Black's fault for their falling-out. When Grandma Black passed away and divided her meager estate between her two children, it had been Kathy who threw a fit heard across three counties. Grandma Mabel had been living in Butte, and most of the caretaking fell on Riley's parents, or so Kathy led everyone to believe. The truth was, Riley and her brother Baxter were the ones who provided the care. Somehow in Kathy's mind, that was as good as her doing it herself. When it came time to divvy up the estate, Kathy demanded the lion's share for her husband, given he was the one living in town.

While Aunt Maisey didn't give a care one way or the other, the will was ironclad, and the money was divided. How a measly five thousand dollars could destroy a family, Riley didn't understand. How a man like Michael Black could allow his wife to have such control was another puzzle, but from that time forward, no one was allowed to talk to Maisey or Dalton. Riley went rogue and talked to her anyway. She'd stayed in touch with her aunt all these years. That was her secret, one her father kept for her.

"She's doing well."

Maisey walked her over to an empty booth and motioned for her to sit down. "It's such a shame about my brother." She lowered her head and shook it, sending a stray locks falling across her forehead. Maisey tucked it back into the nest. "I wanted to attend his funeral, but Kathy forbid it, so Dalton and I drove out a few weeks later and said our goodbyes."

5

"You left the daisies, didn't you?"

Maisey smiled. "He always called me Maisey Daisy."

"I knew it. I could feel your presence."

"Was it a nice funeral?" Maisey asked.

What could she say? Her stepmother refused to spend a dime of his life insurance on a funeral, so she had him cremated and buried in the box his ashes came in? What good would that do?

"It was a small affair."

Maisey lifted her chin and smiled. "You hungry? The blue-plate special is fish and chips today."

No doubt her nose curled. "No, I'm not hungry." Of course, at that exact time, her stomach let out a grumble that could shake the red pleather seats of the booth.

"Not hungry, huh?" She slid from the booth. "Let me tell Ben to whip you up a plate."

"No," she called out, hoping to stop her aunt from ordering her something she couldn't afford and wasn't likely to eat. She hated to be a pain on her first day in town. Maybe because her stepmother had been such a taker, she'd learned not to ask for anything. "I'm a picky eater."

Aunt Maisey reached over for the menu and set it in front of her. "Choose what you want, sweetheart." She touched Riley's cheek. "You're officially an employee, and all meals are free." She gave her a smile that lit up her eyes.

Riley scanned the offerings, looking for the cheapest item she could afford that didn't contain meat. Her eyes fell on a side salad priced at $1.99. "I don't want to take advantage."

"You can't because you're family."

"Okay, I'll have the side salad, please."

Maisey chewed on the end of her pen. "And what else?"

Riley bit the inside of her cheek. "Umm, I don't...I don't eat meat."

"Vegan or vegetarian?" Her aunt looked at her as if it was a normal question.

Back home, Kathy would have slapped a chicken leg on a plate and told her to live with it.

"Vegetarian."

"Grilled cheese and fries coming up." She looked over her shoulder toward the old man in the corner. "I'm going to see if Doc's order is ready, and I'll be back in a minute." She left Riley staring after her. How different would her life have been if she'd been born to Maisey Black?

While she waited for her aunt to return, she glanced around the room. It was a true diner. Black-and-white checkerboard tiles decorated the floors. A counter with a dozen stools took up one side of the room. A lit glass case showed off the various pies no doubt made from scratch right here in the kitchen.

Framed pictures of Elvis and James Dean covered the walls. Red leather-like booths surrounded the room. In the corner sat a silent jukebox with its lights flashing as if to say, "Look at me."

Riley pulled a quarter from her purse and walked over to the music machine. Like the diner, it was fifties all the way. She found a song that seemed to reflect her emotions. Dropping in the quarter, she picked B-27 and listened to the starting beat of "Ain't That a Shame" because her family's

7

situation was exactly that. A mother who'd abandoned her twins. A dead father. A maternal role model who could make Cinderella's stepmother look like a saint.

She strolled back to her booth, passing Mr. Green Eyes. He looked up and smiled. Her damn knees actually shook.

She mentally chastised herself for that reaction. She hadn't come to Aspen Cove to find a boyfriend. She'd come here to find herself.

CHAPTER TWO

Luke Mosier spent most of his free time in the diner. There weren't many entertainment options in Aspen Cove, but at least here he could fill his stomach at the same time as his mind. Nothing in town happened that didn't get discussed in Maisey's Diner.

He picked up the sugar and let it pour like a waterfall into his cup. His dad used to laugh and tell him to add some coffee to his sugar, but back on M and M Ranch where he'd grown up, the coffee was like tar and a hefty dose of cream and sugar was needed to get it down.

"Did you decide what you wanted, handsome?" Maisey leaned her hip against the table with her order pad in her hand.

"Are you flirting with me again?" He loved to tease her and watch her blush. Maisey gave as good as she got. "What's Ben gonna think?"

She set down her pen and reached up to pinch his cheek. After a good squeeze, she dropped her hand. "Darlin', he doesn't care where I get my appetite as long as I bring it home."

"Fair enough." He peeked around her at the blonde who had arrived a few minutes ago. Maisey had screeched the name Riley loud enough for anyone within a ten-mile radius to hear. "New resident or someone visiting?"

Maisey glanced over her shoulder. "Pretty, isn't she?" She watched him for some kind of reaction.

He'd gotten a brief glimpse of her when she walked by to put a quarter in the jukebox. There was no way he'd tell Maisey that his heart had skipped a beat as the blood flowed to his groin. For all he knew, the girl was Dalton's sister. She didn't look much like him, but then again, Luke didn't look anything like his brother Cade or his sister Trinity. God, he missed those two.

"I didn't notice," he lied.

"Sure you didn't. Like she didn't almost trip over her tongue walking past you."

Had she? He couldn't say, but that was probably because he'd also been trying to get his tongue back into his mouth since she'd walked by. "You know her?" Stupid question. She knew her name, so of course she knew her, but it was a good segue into learning more about the stranger in town.

"Since she was born." Maisey's expression turned all warm and soft. "She's my niece. Just pulled into town."

"Hope she enjoys her visit." He knew a beautiful girl like Riley wasn't an Aspen Cove keeper. Not many young, pretty, single women wanted to live in a small town where the nearest manicure was an hour away and Starbucks' monthly specialties were only something you read about and never tasted. Luke looked down at the menu, trying to cover up the smile on his face. It wasn't often there was a new girl in town. With the recent growth and all the construction happening in Aspen Cove, the men outnumbered the women two to one. "I'll have the double cheeseburger and fries, please."

"You want me to introduce you?"

His head shook before the no could come out. "No, thanks. I'm good." He didn't do temporary. He'd had enough one-night stands in Denver to satisfy the busiest gigolo. Nope, at thirty-four, Luke was looking for forever, and she'd have to be something pretty damn special. As the fire chief of the Aspen Cove Fire Department, he had big responsibilities. His woman would have to be tough and confident. She needed to be the type of woman who would love the community like it was her family. As a public servant, he was married to everyone, so his wife would be, too.

Maisey picked up her pen. "Double with fries coming up." She turned but stopped. "Meg said when you came in to tell you hello." Maisey shook her head. "That girl has it bad for you."

Luke rubbed his temples with one hand. Meg had been after him since the day he drove into town. "Thanks for passing on the message."

"Not your type, huh?"

It wasn't his style to dish about anyone. He wasn't past listening to gossip, but he never spread it. Meg had it bad for him, but the way he heard it, she had it bad for anyone with an X and Y chromosome and a job.

"I don't have a type."

Maisey laughed. He loved the way her whole body shook when she did. It was the sign of a woman who went all in. He glanced at Riley, who seemed to be staring off into space. Did that trait run in her family?

"Everyone has a type."

He cocked his head and shrugged. "My first prerequisite is that they're breathing."

She reached forward and tapped his head with her pen. "You set the bar pretty low."

"Not really. I'm not dating Meg." *Oops.* That came out without thought. "I meant to say I'm picky about who I date."

"Mm-hmm." She spun around on her white loafers, the rubber soles squeaking against the checkerboard tiles.

While he waited, he shot off a text to his brother Cade.

Checking in. How's life in Wyoming?

After his father left M and M Ranch, Luke had joined the fire department in Denver. His brother and father had moved to the McKinley Ranch in Wyoming, and Trinity had headed south to Texas, where she'd heard everything was bigger and better.

His phone pinged with an incoming message.

It's about as exciting as watching an inch-worm cross the street. What about you?

Cade was four years younger. Trinity was two years behind him. It was right after she was born that their mom decided ranchers and ranch life wasn't for her. She divorced their dad and moved down to Florida, eventually married a man who owned a night club, and had two more kids.

New girl in town. Things are looking up.

He could almost see his brother laughing.

How many available women does that make? Two or three?

Contrary to popular belief, there were a lot more single women in town than people realized. The problem was, most were under ten or over fifty.

Even at three, that's three more than you have in Wyoming. Those sheep are looking sexy about now, right?

He waited for his brother to reply. All that came through was an emoji flipping him off. He missed that asshole.

Maisey swung by and dropped his food off before she moved to Riley's table with her meal. He lifted his head to see what she was eating. He never liked a woman who couldn't eat. Was never attracted to the type of woman who nibbled on carrots and only drank sparkling water. Real women had curves. Their asses should overflow a man's hand. Their thighs should cradle his hips.

When he saw the grilled cheese sandwich and fries, he smiled. With a meal like that, he bet under that tent of an outfit, she was hiding delicious curves.

He had finished half of his meal when Dalton breezed into the diner and took a look around. A stranger might think he was robbing the place. He was a character straight out of a *Sons of Anarchy* episode. His arms were covered in tattoos, and he wore a black bandana with skulls and crossbones.

What people didn't realize was Dalton was as tame as a kitten but could turn into a lion if those he cared about were threatened.

Riley's eyes opened wide, and a smile as big as a canyon brightened her face. Dalton nodded toward her. "I'll be right there."

Rather than head straight to his cousin, he stopped by Luke's table. "Hey, man, we're having a big bonfire on the beach tonight in front of the house. Could use a fireman... or a friend. Samantha and I would love to have you and the guys over. She's getting so excited about the concert and photo shoot coming up."

"I'll be there."

"See you then."

Luke hadn't known Dalton before Samantha came into his life, but he was grateful she did; otherwise, he'd be working in a Denver suburb instead of Aspen Cove. Samantha White, who was also known as Indigo, was one of the most popular pop stars on record.

On a sabbatical, she'd tried to hide out in Aspen Cove. That's how she met Dalton. When her house burned down and she realized the town only had a volunteer fire department and no truck, she held a concert to fund the Aspen Cove Fire Department. It was one of the only privately funded departments in the state. At the end of each summer, she held a concert in the area to keep it funded. Currently, the department wouldn't need another dime for ten years, but Luke loved that she wanted to secure its future, which in turn secured his future and that of his men.

This year, she was holding a photo shoot. It was a joint project between Poppy Bancroft the photographer, Charlie Whatley the town veterinarian, and Samantha. They wanted to sell firefighter and puppy calendars. How could they refuse? Since they didn't have enough staff to cover twelve months, the town voted on the volunteer firefighters who would grace the pages. Bobby Williams, who was injured in the last fire, would be Mr. August. It was the eighth month, which represented his eight kids. That man was busy. Bowie Bishop would be Mr. July, but he insisted his army buddy Trig Whatley pose with him. Having both served in the United States military, it seemed appropriate to give them independence month. Cannon Bishop got March because his wife Sage reminded everyone of a leprechaun. Doc Parker, also injured in the fire, took on December because he was like Father Christmas to each person in town. He refused to go topless, saying it wouldn't be fair to the rest of them if he showed his over seven decades of finely tuned flab.

The rest of the months were divided up amongst the full and part-time staff. Somehow, he ended up with February. Something told him Meg had voted more than once to put him on the Valentine's spread.

He took a glance at the corner booth where Dalton and Riley were catching up. Her whole demeanor had changed with his appearance. She'd once sat quietly, looking sullen, but was now animated. The color in her cheeks and sparkle in her eyes were captivating.

Luke finished his meal. He'd considered introducing himself but changed his mind. Maybe she'd be at the bonfire

15

later. He took out a twenty and set it on the table before he left. Yep, things might actually be looking up. He walked outside and passed by an old, beat-up Jeep that looked like it belonged to a damn hoarder. At the end of summer, with so many tourists coming through town, it could be anyone.

He peeked inside the dirty windows and saw the tanks of compressed gas and nearly blew his cool. What idiot would travel with compressed gas? The car was like a moving bomb. He marched across the street to the bakery and took a sticky note from the wishing wall. The wall was a local tradition started by Katie the bakery owner. People would come in for a muffin and write a wish on a yellow sticky note. Everyone pitched in to grant the reasonable wishes. Last week, he'd helped old man Meyers paint his house. Too bad he couldn't wish for the end of stupidity. It looked like he'd have to tackle the problem one idiot at a time. On the note, he wrote, *If you don't care about yourself, think about others. Traveling with compressed gas is stupid, stupid, stupid.*

He stuck it to the driver's side window and left.

CHAPTER THREE

Riley finished the last bite of her grilled cheese and drank her coffee while Dalton sat across from her and spoke of how happy he was to have her in town.

"I'm happy to be here." She looked around the diner at the life they'd made for themselves. It hadn't been easy for Maisey or Dalton. Maybe the Blacks were cursed with bad luck. Between the abuse from Maisey's ex-husband and Dalton's prison sentence for killing a man, they'd been to hell and back, but as she looked around the diner, she saw what hope and perseverance could do. They'd made it out of hell and were sitting on a nice piece of heaven. Maybe she could, too.

"Tell me about Samantha."

Dalton's smile took up his face. "She's amazing. I'm so glad she has poor taste in men."

"Stop." She was the queen of self-deprecation. She'd

learned how to perfect it from years of hearing everything that was wrong with her, but she hated to hear others speak poorly of themselves. "You're a great catch. Who doesn't like a man who can cook? How's the culinary school going?"

"It's turned into more of a take and bake, but I've got a few regulars who stop in for lessons. Cannon, who you'll meet later, sends Sage twice a month. I'd never met a woman who couldn't boil water until her. Basil Dawson comes in once a week and tries his hand at cooking. He's become quite the quiche maker. Big cowboy who rides the range all day, only to spend his free time making something as delicate as a quiche."

"You never know what's brewing inside a person until you set them free." Riley was ready to be emancipated. She needed to find out what she was capable of doing on her own but was scared she'd fail. If she did, what then? It wasn't like she had anywhere else to go. Returning to Butte wasn't an option. She'd never go back to the place that had molded her into someone she didn't want to be.

"What's inside of you that's waiting to be freed?" Dalton leaned back and crossed his arms behind his head.

"I'm a work in progress."

She stared at his tattoos. His arms were covered in sleeves that told the story of his life. She bet if given enough time, she could find every success and failure etched into his skin. She reached behind her and touched the scar on her back. She too bore the scars of life, only she didn't choose hers.

"Let's get you started. Finish up here, and I'll meet you around the back of the bakery across the street to help you unload your stuff. Give me about ten minutes to get there." He was up and out of the booth before she could say another word.

Maisey walked over and took Dalton's place. "I've got you scheduled tomorrow for your first shift."

Riley had never waitressed before, so she was nervous. "What if I'm a terrible server?"

Maisey laughed. "Can you talk and write?"

Riley knew she was trying to ease her fear. "Not at the same time, but yep, I can do those two things."

"Can you walk and carry a plate or two?" She reached forward and stacked the silverware and empty glass on top of the plate.

"Yes, I'm pretty sure I've got walking mastered, and I'll figure out the plate carrying."

"You'll make a fine waitress. Show everyone that pretty smile of yours, and you'll be great. The tips will be pouring in."

The bell above the door rang, and a woman in her late twenties to early thirties bounced in. She played up the fifties theme with her pink waitress uniform and black and white saddle shoes. She looked around the mostly empty diner, and when her eyes lighted on Maisey, she hurried over.

"Hey Maise, is this the new girl?" She smiled like a woman trying to win a trophy.

"Yep, this is Riley." Maisey looked past her to where the old man she'd called Doc sat. "I've got to cash Doc out. Why don't you introduce yourself to my niece?"

Maisey left, and the woman took her seat. "I'm Meg. I'll be training you."

"Hi, Meg. I fear I'm in for a big learning curve. I've never waitressed."

Meg stared at her without saying a word. She took her in from the top of her head to where her body hid behind the table. "There's nothing to it, really. The key is to smile a lot and flirt. We have many single men in town, and they have deep pockets for a girl with a nice smile." She looked down to where the buttons of her dress were opened to reveal a large amount of cleavage. "Don't forget to show your personality."

Riley wasn't sure what she meant, but with the way Meg looked at her girls, she was pretty certain they were what she'd dubbed as personality.

"Umm, do I have to wear a uniform?"

Meg giggled. "No, this is my thing. I like to play the part. I'm good at it." She swung her head back and forth, and her long brown ponytail swished in the air. "Remember to smile. You may want to murder someone on the inside, but you get more tips with sugar than salt."

Riley was sure the saying was something like *you get more flies with honey than vinegar,* but it never made much sense because why would someone want flies? In her experience, the saying meant you'll have more success luring people into a trap by being nice than by being mean. She was well-versed in that bait and switch. Kathy used kindness to manipulate situations. Riley fell for it all the time because she thought maybe once, her stepmother was truly being nice.

She looked at Meg and decided she didn't have any

reason not to trust her motives, and if a smile and cleavage brought her some sugar, or in this case tips, she was game to try anything.

"It was nice meeting you. I look forward to learning from you." She looked past her to the window. "I'm supposed to meet Dalton in a few minutes, but I'll catch you tomorrow." She looked down at the empty plate topped with her glass and silverware. "Is there someplace I can put this?"

Meg smiled. "No, sweetie. I can take care of it. That's what friends are for."

Riley wondered if that was possible. Could it be that easy to adjust to a new place? Could she meet someone new and have a friend for life?

"Thanks. I could use a friend." She slid out of the booth. She caught her aunt's eyes and pointed to the door. Maisey waved at her and told her she'd see her tomorrow.

Riley had walked into the diner feeling pensive and walked out feeling powerful. She had a new life. Things were going to be different for her. She'd no longer be a whipping boy to others. She was a strong, capable woman who had a lot to offer the world. She might not be the prettiest or the skinniest or the most talented, but she was something, and it was her greatest desire to find out what that something was.

When she rounded her Jeep to the driver's side, she smiled at the yellow note stuck to her window. No doubt it was a note from Dalton, or maybe Maisey had snuck out and left it for her. Her heart felt warm and full until she read it.

If you don't care about yourself, think about others. Traveling with compressed gas is stupid, stupid, stupid.

She stood there with her mouth agape and read it again. She'd been in town less than an hour, and someone had stepped in to take Kathy's place. She fisted the note and gritted her teeth. Aspen Cove was supposed to be different.

She opened the door and tossed the note to the floorboard. Maybe what needed to be different was her.

She turned the key and waited for the Jeep to shake and shudder to life. Thankful it started again, she pulled it around the back of the bakery, where Dalton stood outside talking to a group of men.

She stepped out of the SUV and leaned against the door, waiting.

"Riley, come meet my friends."

He introduced her to Bowie, Trig and Cannon. She took the handsome men in. They weren't as good looking as Mr. Green Eyes, but Aspen Cove sure did breed beautiful.

Once the introductions were over, the men disappeared. Dalton opened the back of her SUV. "Is this all your baggage?"

If we're talking emotional baggage, I left that in Butte.

She looked at the single suitcase and milk crate that had a few of her favorite things, like the erector set that had gotten her an ass whoopin' all those years ago.

"I travel light."

He looked to where she'd managed to squeeze two welders and all the supplies she could fit into her vehicle.

"There's nothing light about that load." He picked up her suitcase. "We can take stuff to the studio tomorrow." He stared at the gas cylinders. "Those empty?"

She thought about the note left on her window. "Yes. I'd be stupid, stupid, stupid to drive with full tanks in an enclosed, unstable environment."

"It's a good thing you're a Black, because one thing we're not is stupid."

While she wanted to agree with him, she couldn't. She'd done a lot of stupid things in her day but moving to Aspen Cove seemed like she was bucking that trend.

"Lead the way." She picked up the milk crate and followed him into the back door of the bakery.

"This used to open into the bakery, but Katie had a door put in so you can have a private entrance." He pointed up the steep staircase. "You're at the top of the stairs."

They walked up, and Dalton opened the door.

Riley didn't know what to expect. All she knew was, today was the first moment of the rest of her life. When she entered the apartment, she smiled. It looked like maybe, just maybe she was getting a piece of heaven too.

Dalton gave her a quick tour. "There's a bonfire at my house on the beach. Come early to meet Samantha, Katie, and Sage."

She wanted to tell her cousin she was going to pass, but she didn't have the heart to dismiss his hospitality. "Can I bring anything?" While she offered, she prayed he'd say no because she had nothing to offer except a few cans of vegetarian chili she had tucked behind her seat and the case of Ramen noodles on the floorboard in front of the passenger seat.

"Bring yourself. It's your welcome party, although we

don't need a reason to celebrate. Life is good here. You'll figure that out soon enough."

He kissed her cheek and disappeared down the stairs, leaving Riley alone for the first time.

She walked through the apartment slowly by herself. It was perfect. Two bedrooms and two bathrooms. Fully furnished, it smelled sweet, like honey. She walked over to the window and stared out at the town below her.

People milled about, and she watched a woman with eight children enter the corner store. The old man who had been at the diner walked out and moved toward the pharmacy and clinic. A pregnant woman stepped out of the veterinary clinic and made her way across the street. A few minutes later, she returned with a bag in her hand. Riley smiled, thinking she'd picked up treats from the bakery below.

The smell of chocolate and coffee wafted through the floorboards and filled her space with the smell of love. At least it smelled like love to her. Brownies and cookies were her go-to when she needed to feel love.

When she got to the kitchen, she found a note on the table and a plate of love in the shape of cookies, muffins and double chocolate brownies.

Welcome to Aspen Cove!

I put some staples in the refrigerator. I'm so happy to have you as a neighbor. Feel free to visit the bakery anytime. Coffee and muffins are on the house. It's a perk for living upstairs. I'll see you at the bonfire tonight.

Katie and Bowie and Sahara and Bishop.

She smiled at the note and picked up a cookie. She took a

bite and moaned at the sweet peanut buttery taste. All she needed was a glass of milk to make it perfect. She opened the fridge and cried. Inside, the shelves were filled with juice and fruit and vegetables and a gallon of milk. There was a package of meat she'd make sure to give back, but outside of that, she was set for a week or more. Never in her whole life had she felt this kind of welcome. Not in her hometown. Not in her home.

She wiped her tears, poured herself a glass of milk then sat by the window and looked out at her new life. The town, the people, the apartment, the cookie, the milk. It was all perfect. One thing was certain, Riley was determined to bury the old and start a new life here.

CHAPTER FOUR

Luke parked outside the bed and breakfast and walked between Sage and Cannon's house and Katie and Bowie's place. Up the shore, he saw the flames of the bonfire flicker in the waning light.

The autumn air was brisk at night, and he was glad the fire was fully engaged. It would warm them up when the temperature dropped into the forties, like it often did in the mountains. He searched the crowd for Riley but didn't see her. He wasn't sure if he was disappointed or relieved. One thing was for certain, he was torn. She was attractive but temporary. Maybe temporary wasn't such a bad thing after all. It could certainly make his nights less lonely.

He looked over his shoulder at the homes lit along the shoreline. All his friends lived in these houses. They were either married or close to it. The holdouts were Samantha and Dalton, but that was more logistics than anything else.

She spent a good deal of time on the road, so it was hard to pin a day down. The latest news was, she was done touring for the year and would be recording at the studio she'd built at the Guild Creative Center. That meant there would be an influx of people coming to Aspen Cove for the winter. Her band would arrive next month, along with her assistant.

Luke wondered if that would change the dynamics of the town. New people were arriving all the time. He both hated it and loved it. With growth came change. The last being a pretty thing named Riley. He wasn't sure if her arrival was something to celebrate or dread.

"You want a beer?" Thomas stepped away from the fire and pulled a bottle from the open cooler beside him.

It came rushing at Luke like an arrow, but his reflexes were good. He twisted off the cap and pocketed it to toss in a trash can later. "When did you get here?" Thomas helped man the fire station. He was as close to a deputy as Luke had. He came over from Silver Springs, so he was familiar with the mountain landscape.

"Someone had to make sure the fire was safe." He watched the flames lick several feet into the air.

"Leave it to a firefighter to build an inferno."

Thomas lifted his bottle in a toast. "Go big or go home."

"Speaking of home, have you found a place of your own?" Thomas had been bunking at the fire station. It was equipped to sleep six, but it wasn't a home. Most of the crew had places of their own. Thomas was the holdout, looking for something that would serve him long-term.

"I've got it narrowed down to two places. One on

Hyacinth, and one on Pansy. I'm leaning toward the first place because I can't bring myself to live on a street called Pansy."

Luke laughed. "I live on Bark Lane."

Thomas took a long drink of his beer. "Yeah, but you're not committed for life. It's a rental, right?"

Luke nodded. "Can't decide if I want to live in town or get a ranch." He knew he was going to stay in Aspen Cove, but he wasn't certain where he wanted to plant roots. He took a glance at the lot behind them. Not too long ago, there was a cabin there, but an arsonist had sent it up in flames. Samantha owned the land, and Luke wondered if she planned to add on to the house where she and Dalton lived, or if she'd consider selling the lot. Land like that wouldn't come cheap, but it would be worth it. Waking up to the sun glinting off the lake each morning would be amazing.

"I hear we have a new hottie in town." A few more of the team crowded around Thomas the minute he mentioned a new woman. In a town where men outnumbered the ladies, a new, pretty face was like hitting the lottery or finding a unicorn.

Luke didn't care for the interest that was being shown to Riley's arrival. He hadn't traded any words with her yet, but somewhere deep inside, he didn't want someone else to swoop her up before he got a chance to meet her.

"Speak of the devil," Thomas said and nodded toward Dalton's house. Dressed in the same flowing white skirt and top was Riley. She'd walked out of Dalton's house laughing with Samantha.

James, the youngest of the group, let out a low whistle. "That's no devil. You see the white? She's an angel."

Thomas tapped the bottom of his jaw. "Close your mouth before you drool."

The group fell silent as Riley and Samantha passed.

Luke turned to look at her and found her staring back at him. Her eyes were as blue as a robin's eggs. Not even the sunset could steal their beauty. When a hint of a smile curved her lips, his lungs ceased to work. When his heart boomed in his chest, he was reminded that nothing worked without oxygen, and he inhaled deeply. There was a hint of citrus on the air. Was it her or someone else? She spun around when Sage and Katie approached.

"Earth to Luke," Thomas said.

He shook his head and faced his team. James pretended to wipe Luke's chin. "Looks like I'm not the only one salivating over the new girl in town. Who is she?"

"That is Riley Black," he said.

"As in Dalton's sister?" Thomas tossed his empty bottle into a nearby trash can. "Damn, it's a good thing she doesn't look like him."

Luke shook his head. "She's his cousin."

"Damn," James added. "I wonder what she's hiding under that skirt."

Luke had the same thoughts, but he kept them private. "Watch it," he warned. "You're a public servant, a pillar of the community, people look up to you. Act respectable."

James laughed. "Don't tell me you weren't thinking the same thing."

"Thinking is different than saying. Mind your manners."

He took a drink and turned around to catch another glimpse of Riley, but she was gone. A crowd of locals was filling up the beach and the buffet table. Soon, it would be hard to find her anywhere. One thing about Aspen Cove was, they loved their potlucks and bonfires.

Luke decided to change the focus of the conversation from women to work.

"Keep your eyes open. Looks like the latest idiot has come into town."

"Worse than Tilden Cool?"

No one was worse than Tilden Cool. He made lazy look downright criminal. In fact, in most places what Tilden Cool did would be considered criminal, but not in Colorado. He helped old man Tucker make moonshine. They couldn't sell it because that was illegal, but they bartered it for stuff they needed, like groceries and services. He'd already put out three still fires since he arrived.

"Could be worse. Some idiot driving a Jeep came into town with oxygen and acetylene tanks in the back seat. Worse yet, they left them in the car with only the window cracked open a hair's width."

"You're kidding."

"No, I'm serious. I came out of the diner, and there it was. A piece of shit car that probably rolled in on a prayer and was filled with junk and gas tanks."

Thomas shook his head. "That's the problem with being a private hire. We don't have the authority to enforce. All you can do is talk to Aiden or Mark and hope they can track down the owner."

Luke tossed his empty bottle into the trash can.

"I left a note. It may not be a summons, but I hope it gets the message across." He shoved his hands in his pockets. While he wanted to grab another beer, he had a one drink limit. "What I wanted to do was take whoever the idiot was behind the tool shed for an ass beating and a lesson in safety."

He waited for his crew to chime in, but they were all silent. Their eyes focused behind him. Someone tapped his shoulder, and he turned around to meet the stare of Riley.

"Hey," he said and pulled his hands from his pockets. "I'm Luke Mosier."

He offered his hand, which she took in hers.

"I'm the idiot. When should we schedule my public flogging?"

CHAPTER FIVE

Riley thought the handsome man would be a nice distraction on a tough day, but holy hell, she never expected him to be the person who'd left the note. What was even more surprising was her comeback. She rarely, if ever, stood up for herself, but here she was standing in front of a man who was no less than half a foot taller than her, and she'd actually confronted him.

He stood there holding her hand, which wasn't unpleasant given his demeanor. Who would have thought the man with the pretty green eyes could spill such vitriol from those kissable lips?

"I'm sorry you heard that." He looked down at where his hand had completely covered hers and let go.

"Are you sorry?"

He shifted back and forth on his feet. Behind him, several men stood watching—waiting to see what would happen.

He glanced over his shoulder then turned back, pinning her in place with his gemstone eyes.

"No, I'm not sorry. As the town's fire chief, it's my duty to make sure those around here aren't posing a safety issue for others."

"I'm a safety issue?" She didn't know what to do with her hands. Fisted up at her sides, she wanted to lash out and sock him in the nose. "I'm a pacifist. I'd never do anything to harm anyone." Funny how a word with fist in it meant she'd never use hers. How many times had she closed her eyes and imagined defending herself? But in the end, she'd lowered her head, apologized and walked away. Not today.

"You endanger the entire town by driving a mobile bomb. Do you have any idea what could happen if someone hit your car? If the tanks got jostled around and became unstable, or what would happen if they overheated?" He balled his hands together and pulled them apart, adding in explosive sound effects. "You'd be hamburger meat."

He had good points if in fact she had been an idiot, but she was weak, not stupid, and standing in front of him and being admonished for something she wasn't guilty of felt too reminiscent of her life in Butte.

Her brother always told her she had no backbone and that was a problem. It was why at twenty-seven, she had still lived near her parents. The truth was, what she lacked in backbone, she made up for in heart. There was no way she'd abandon her father. Leaving him with Kathy was like leaving a cat in charge of the parakeet—uncaged.

She stood up to her full five foot five inches and pulled

back her shoulders. She shook out her hair and smiled. The smile was the best defense against tears.

"You said Luke, right?" She stared up at him.

"Yes, Luke Mosier."

She took a step back. Wasn't sure if it was a step for her or for him. She didn't know him and therefore didn't know what he was capable of doing.

"Mr. Mosier, I'm not the idiot you assumed I am. In fact, I'm versed on how to travel with flammable materials, and I can assure you those tanks were in fact purged prior to my travels. Only an idiot would carry unsecured fuel tanks inside a car."

He shoved his hands back in his pockets and turned around to face the men still standing and staring behind him.

"Don't you have beer to drink or a fire to tend?"

A man as big as Luke stepped forward. "Nope, boss, we're enjoying the show. This is a good lesson for the boys to learn. Nothing like on-the-job training on how to deal with... what did he call you?"

Riley smiled. She liked the man in front of her. Liked the way he pushed Luke's buttons. Liked the way he put him on the spot. There was no fear from him even though it was apparent he was talking to his boss.

"An idiot."

The man stepped forward and held out his hand for her to shake. "I'm Thomas, and if all idiots were as pretty as you, we'd be happy to have a townful, but something tells me you're not as stupid as he claims." He turned to Luke. "Carry on with the lesson, boss."

Luke looked at her and pointed toward the empty lot. "Can I speak to you in private?"

She shook her head. "I don't think so. You called me an idiot in public, and I feel it's my right to defend myself in front of the masses."

She looked around and noticed several people had moved closer, their eyes focused on the showdown.

"Fine. You and I both know if those tanks had in fact been purged, they would have been tagged accordingly. Given they held no tags, I can only deduce you're not being completely honest."

She looked around at the faces and saw they had already convicted her of a crime she hadn't committed. She had hoped her experience in Aspen Cove would be different than what she'd grown up with in Butte. Why did one person's opinion become fact?

It was time to set the record straight once and for all. If she was going to have a life here, people needed to know who she was, not who someone else told them she was.

"I drive a Jeep that is, in fact, a piece of crud, but it got me here. I coasted into town on fumes and luck. It was an eleven-hour trip in temperatures that reached the nineties. Not pleasant without air conditioning. Have you ever listened to a tag flap in the wind caused from open windows?" She paused until he nodded. "Then you'll understand why I removed the tags." She reached down and grabbed a beer from the open cooler. "I think you owe me this and an apology."

Riley didn't wait for the apology because in her experience they never came, so she spun around and looked through the crowd for a friendly face.

Standing next to the water, she saw Samantha, Sage and the pregnant woman she'd watched cross the street earlier.

She popped the top on her beer and walked over to join them.

"What was that all about?" Samantha asked.

"Oh, you know, making new friends." She'd met Sage a few minutes before the confrontation. "Did you say you owned the bed and breakfast?" In her experience, it was always better to get people talking about themselves. It drew the attention away from her.

"Yep." She pointed over her shoulder to the place with the big deck where everyone was dropping off dishes of food. "I also work as a nurse for Doc Parker and my sister, Lydia Covington."

"Wow, you obviously keep busy."

Samantha laughed. "She's like a leaping leprechaun. She's in a ton of places at once. If you don't see her here or the clinic, she's drawing pints at the bar."

"Says the woman who tours, builds centers for the arts and a fire station."

"Don't forget I'm holding a concert next month and starting a new album."

The pregnant woman rested her hands on her belly. "I'm baking two babies. I'm not that busy."

All three of the women next to Riley laughed.

Sage added, "Oh, and running the veterinary clinic and putting up with Trig."

"I met him earlier today, along with Bowie. He seems nice."

The young woman beamed. "I'm Charlie, and Trig is my husband and baby daddy. Doc is my father."

"Seems like you're getting acquainted with the best Aspen Cove has to offer," Samantha said.

"I'm definitely meeting people, that's for sure. Is Katie around?"

They all turned to look at the house behind them.

"She's probably trying to get Sahara down for the night. She'd be your niece, I think."

Riley thought about it. If her Aunt Maisey was married to Ben and he was Bowie's father and Bowie was Katie's husband, that would make Sahara her first cousin once removed. She hadn't considered Katie was actually family by marriage.

"She's been kind to me, giving me a place to stay, and I wanted to thank her for such a generous gift."

Even in the duskiness of the approaching night, she could see the smiles on everyone's face. It was Sage who spoke next.

"It's the way of Aspen Cove. The town is the gift that keeps on giving."

Riley opened her eyes wide. "That could be said of herpes too."

All three women looked at her before they broke into laughter.

Riley looked around to see if anyone else had heard her. She sometimes came out with the strangest analogies. Had no idea where her brain pulled those quips from. The townsfolk had paid her no mind, but she did catch the glint of green eyes watching her from afar. Luke stared in her direction, never taking his eyes off her. She could almost feel the heat of the fire reflecting from the flames of his eyes to hers. The warmth that filled her body was a cross between irritation and attraction. More so irritation at herself for being attracted to such a jerk.

Sage proceeded to tell her how a woman named Bea Bishop had given her the bed and breakfast and had given Katie the bakery. They felt it was their responsibility to pay it forward.

"Even if you hadn't been family, you would have been taken care of, because we take care of our own. You're Maisey's, so that makes you ours too."

For the second time since she arrived in Aspen Cove, she felt welcomed. Standing next to three women who appreciated her presence was almost as good as the hug from her aunt—almost as good as how Luke's warm hand felt wrapped around hers.

CHAPTER SIX

Luke woke up with a headache. Not the kind a person gets from drinking too much beer, but the kind from thinking too hard and not sleeping enough.

"Because you're pissed at yourself doesn't mean you have to punish the rest of us," James complained.

"It's Saturday. We always polish the rig on Saturday. Stop complaining." Luke believed nice things stayed nice if they received tender loving care. Every weekend, whoever was on shift got to wash the truck and make it shine.

"What's the point? You make us get it all clean and shiny, then you allow the kids to climb all over it." Jacob was another youngster. He'd come to Aspen Cove from Copper Creek. He was a highly motivated man until it came to sponges and soap.

"We are role models to these kids. They see you work

hard and share the fruits of your labor. It's important to build community relationships."

Thomas rounded the corner with a mug of coffee. He wasn't on shift today, but since he bunked at the station, he was always around.

"Is that what you call that interaction with the hottie last night? Were you building a relationship by publicly humiliating the woman?"

"Drop it. I feel bad about calling her an idiot, but until I see those tags, which I'm sure will never surface, I'm not buying her story."

"I believe her," James piped in.

"Me too," added Jacob.

Luke looked at Thomas. "You want to bust my balls too?"

He shook his head. "Nope, but I'll stand back and watch her do it."

"Never going to happen. She openly admitted to being a pacifist."

"Was that what she said? I thought for sure she said if you didn't shut up, she was going to pass a fist... straight to your face." Thomas shrugged and walked away.

Tired of listening to them tease about last night, he threw the soft cloth he was using to buff the stainless steel into the nearby bucket.

"You finish up. I'm going to grab breakfast."

There was a collective groan.

"We want breakfast too," James said.

"There's a box of muffins in the kitchen. Courtesy of Katie."

One of the things he loved about the town was they looked out after each other. The bakery set out a box of muffins daily for the fire department and police department. Often, they'd get a knock on the door and find a local delivering a casserole or batch of cookies. No place did friendly like Aspen Cove.

Luke felt a pang of regret about the way he treated Riley. While she had been in the wrong, he didn't have to use such strong language. He could have simply told her the dangers and asked her to rectify the problem, but he called her an idiot, which made him feel like one.

After a hearty meal at the diner, he figured he'd track her down and help her take care of the tanks. It would be the responsible thing to do.

Maisey rushed by with two plates of bacon and eggs balancing in one hand and the pot of coffee swinging from the other.

"Mornin', Luke. I'll be right there with coffee."

He glanced around and found the front corner booth he loved was still open. Saturdays were busy in the diner. Tourists and locals alike came for Dalton and Ben's waffles and pancakes. The batter was smooth as silk and slightly sweet. Pair that with real maple syrup and a dab of butter, and it was heaven served on a plate.

He looked around the room to see familiar faces. Doc sat on the other side of the diner with his girlfriend, Agatha. Luke wondered if the old couple would ever marry. In the large corner booth were Bobby and Louise Williams with their eight children.

Maisey whizzed over and filled up his mug. "Cakes or waffle?" she asked.

"Waffle with double bacon."

"You got it." She was gone in a flash.

The bell above the door rang, and Dalton walked inside. He split his time between the diner and his culinary school, which was closed on the weekends.

As he always did, he walked inside and looked at the place the way Luke figured a criminal cased the yard. Dalton was always on alert. He figured it must be inbred in him after spending years in prison. As soon as he saw Luke in the corner, he headed his way.

"Cakes or waffles?" He slid into the booth across from Luke.

"Went for waffles. I thought you'd be in the back making them."

Dalton moved farther into the booth and leaned against the wall, kicking his feet up on the bench. "Nope. I've got a few things to take care of today."

Luke didn't know how to approach the subject of Dalton's cousin, so he dove in. "I met Riley last night at the bonfire."

Dalton smiled like he was her father. There was a glimmer of pride that showed in the twinkle of his eyes. "I'm so glad she's here."

Luke doctored his coffee with a heavy dose of sugar and a splash of cream. "What's her story?"

With a wave of his hand, Dalton pointed to a half-dozen

people in the diner. "Her story is everyone's story. She's looking for a place to belong."

Luke dropped his spoon, and the clank caught the attention of a few diners nearby. "She's staying?" That made things even worse, because now he'd have to see her all the time and know he was the first person in the town to make her feel unwelcome. It wasn't one of his finer moments. He still stood behind his position about the tanks, but he could have been nicer delivering the message.

"She moved here." He turned to look over his shoulder toward the window. "She's staying above the bakery for now, but once her art takes off, and I know it will, she'll be looking for something more permanent."

"Her art?"

"She's a metal sculptor. Samantha is giving her studio space so she can work. She had it rough in Butte. She's a real Cinderella story, except her stepmother makes Lady Tremaine look like a saint."

"How in the hell do you know Cinderella's stepmother's name?"

A pink blush colored Dalton's cheeks. "It played a lot in the rec room. I've pretty much got the script memorized, all the way from Anastasia and Drizella to Gus the mouse."

"I'm not sure if I should be impressed or concerned." He sipped his coffee and added more sugar. "One thing is for certain, you're going to make some little girl an awesome father."

"You know it, but my daughter isn't dating until she's thirty."

"Sounds like you're in the planning stages."

"Always try to stay one step ahead. What about you? You're a decent looking guy with a job. When are you going to find someone?" It took all of a minute for Dalton to ponder his own words. "Oh wait… is that why you're asking about my cousin?"

Luke knew where he was going with it. His head was moving from side to side before the words could come out. "No. In fact, I'd be lucky if she gave me the time of day. I kind of pissed her off."

"Way to go, slick." The bell above the door rang. "Speak of the devil."

"My crew says she resembles an angel." Luke watched Riley walk inside. She looked nervous as she moved slowly into the center of the room. Dressed in blue jeans and a plaid shirt tied at her waist, she was downright adorable.

Dalton tapped the table to get Luke's attention. "I've got to go. It's my job to get her settled in, but I'll catch you later." He slid out of the booth and stood looking down at Luke. "Be nice to her, because I don't want to go back to jail if I have to kick your ass. I like you, man, but family comes first." He turned and approached Riley. Instead of hugging her, Dalton picked her up and spun her in a big circle. She squealed with laughter.

When he put her down, she quickly looked around the diner. When her eyes lit on Luke, her smile turned into a thin-lipped scowl.

A plate plopped on the table in front of him. He turned

his attention from Riley to the waffle and bacon in front of him.

"Thanks, Maisey."

"Look again."

He'd recognize that voice anywhere. "Sorry, Meg. Maisey took my order, and I wasn't paying attention."

She looked over her shoulder toward Dalton and Riley. "You were looking at something, or maybe someone?"

"No, not really. Just kind of in a daze."

She plopped into the booth across from him. "Anything you could want is right in front of you." She smiled wide, and he saw her red lipstick had rubbed off on her teeth.

"You're right. All I want now is bacon and this waffle." He looked up at her and hoped she got the message.

"That's what you think you want, but if you'd only pay attention, you'd see there's so much more waiting for you."

Luke looked around the table. "Right again. Can I get extra butter and syrup?"

Meg groaned. "If you weren't so cute, I'd give up on you."

He wanted to tell her he wished she would but was certain there was a box of rat poison in the back that would find itself in his next meal if he wasn't careful. On the outside, Meg came across as pleasant and nice, but he'd known lots of girls like her. Inside, she was a rabid pitbull waiting to bite.

He filled his mouth with a piece of bacon, ending any further conversation. Meg stormed off and came back moments later to slam the syrup container on the table. Luke shook his head. He was 0-for-2 when it came to women this week.

CHAPTER SEVEN

Her heart thumped loudly. Riley was certain everyone in the diner could hear it. Was her heart racing because she would start a new job today? Was it because Dalton had spun her around like a rag doll, or was it because Luke Mosier was sitting in the corner booth, staring at her?

She shifted so her back was turned to him and focused her attention on Dalton.

"What are you doing here?"

"My mom is going to take off soon with Ben, so I'm taking over the kitchen. I thought I'd come by early and tell you to break a leg."

She glanced back at Luke, who was now focused on his plate. "Does it have to be *my* leg? Can I volunteer someone else's limb?"

Dalton laughed. He wrapped his arm around her shoulders and led her through the swinging doors into the kitchen.

"He said he pissed you off. Hard to believe because he's such a good guy and you have the reputation in the family as being unflappable."

She wasn't as calm as she often seemed. She'd learned long ago to hide her emotions for self-preservation.

"I wouldn't put him in charge of the welcome wagon."

"Riley," Aunt Maisey said as she appeared from around the corner with an older man who could only be Ben, since he was wearing more orange lipstick than her aunt was. Maisey thumbed the smear from his lower lip and smiled. "This is your Uncle Ben."

"Hi, Ben." It was odd to call him her uncle.

Emptiness had filled her soul as she drove out of Montana toward Colorado. She'd left the only family she'd ever known and ventured toward the unfamiliar. Never had she felt so lonely as when she'd pulled into town, but then she found out she wasn't alone. In a matter of a day, her family had grown from Aunt Maisey, Dalton and her brother Baxter to all of them, plus Samantha, Katie, Bowie, Cannon, and baby Sahara.

"I hate to do this to you, but my sweet Ben has surprised me with a romantic trip to Denver." Her aunt winked. "I'll be gone for a few days."

Dalton had already moved to the grill and was flipping pancakes and turning bacon.

"You're going away?" As silly as it sounded, that hollow feeling sank to her gut. "I just got here, and you're already leaving me."

Aunt Maisey gave her one of those mothers looks.

Straight-faced. Narrowed eyes. The kind of look that came with advice.

"You'll be fine. You wanted to come here to find your place in the world. You can't do that hiding in Butte or behind my skirt."

"You're right. It's that everything is so new."

Maisey raised her hand and cupped Riley's cheek. "Sweetheart, in order to belong to someone or someplace, you have to let them have a piece of you. Your job while I'm gone is to become familiar with the town and its people. If you don't venture out of your comfort zone and meet the people, then you'll be in no better shape than you were in Butte."

Her aunt was right but putting herself out there was risky.

Aunt Maisey kissed her. Riley hoped she didn't have the outline of orange lips on her cheek; then again, it was unlikely since Ben was wearing most of the lipstick anyway.

"It's nice to meet you, Riley," Ben said. He turned to Maisey. "You ready, sweetheart?"

Maisey threaded her fingers through Ben's.

"Meg will train you this weekend. By Monday, you'll be a pro."

She stood in the middle of the kitchen and watched her aunt and uncle walk out. A few seconds later, the swinging doors opened, and a wad of fabric hit her in the head.

"Get your apron on. You've got tables waiting," Meg said.

Dalton slid a couple of plates through the window. "Knock 'em dead, Riley."

Her inner brat said she had a list of people she wanted to

clobber, and it was getting longer. After hitting her with a projectile apron, Meg might have jumped to the top.

Riley put her bag where she saw everyone else's stacked on a table to the side and tied the black apron around her waist. She pulled the hair tie from her wrist and wrestled her hair into a ponytail.

I can do this.

She put on a practiced smile and entered the restaurant.

In seconds, Meg put an order pad and pen in her hand and shuffled her toward the corner booth, where Doc Parker sat with a woman she hadn't met.

"They need coffee, and Doc always wants pie."

When Riley stood still for a minute, Meg shifted her hip and gave her a bump forward. "He's easy and a good person to start with."

Riley slowly walked to the table. When she got there, she stopped. Her mouth opened to say hello, but no words came out.

"You must be Riley," the older woman said. "Charlie said she met you last night at the bonfire. I'm Agatha." She moved her hand across the table to lay it over Doc Parker's. "This old fart is Paul, but everyone calls him Doc."

There was no doubt she looked like a woman possessed, with her nodding head and smile. If she had a grass skirt and coconut bra, she'd make a fine dashboard doll.

"Cat got your tongue?" Doc asked. "You don't have to be nervous with us. We're easy."

Riley swallowed the knot in her throat. "Hi, I'm Riley."

Doc chuckled. "I think we established that already. Now is where you ask me what kind of pie I want."

She shook the paralysis from her body. "Right, you want pie." Riley looked toward the pie case to see what was there, but it all looked the same. There were three perfectly baked two crust pies.

"Cherry for me. Apple for Agatha. Give us one scoop of vanilla ice cream to share."

Riley wrote down four words.

Apple

Cherry

Ice Cream

"I'll get that."

She turned around and walked to the pie case. She had no idea what she was doing. Meg was leaning against Luke's table, making sure she got a good tip. Riley swore she'd undone another button for him. She had no interest in the man, but something about Meg blatantly offering her goods didn't sit right with Riley. She didn't want his beautiful green eyes looking at Meg's perfect personality.

"Excuse me," Riley called from across the room. When Meg didn't come to her rescue, she internally cussed up a storm because now she'd be forced to go to Luke's table and prove maybe he was right and she was an idiot.

Not wanting to keep Doc waiting, she swallowed her pride and walked over to Meg.

"I need some help figuring the pie out."

She tried to keep her eyes on Meg, but damnit if his lips

didn't call to her. There were some men who had lips that appeared full and soft like a pillow. Luke had those lips.

"Riley, good to see you again." His words moved over her skin like velvet.

She didn't reply but looked at Meg. "I'll wait for you over there." She about ran to the other side of the diner.

A minute later, Meg sashayed over. There was an exaggerated sway to her hips. When Riley glanced past her to see if Luke was mesmerized, she found him staring at her and not Meg's bountiful booty.

"What's the flavor of the day?" Meg followed her line of sight to Luke. "He's a beautiful man, isn't he?"

Beautiful wasn't the word that came to mind when she looked at Luke. "He's perfect if you value pleasant looks over personality." She grabbed two plates and a small bowl she found sitting nearby. "I need an apple, a cherry and a scoop of vanilla ice cream."

Meg showed her how big to cut the slices. She explained that most diners would divide the pie into eight pieces to get more revenue, but Maisey liked to give her customers more.

Meg stuck a fork on each plate and put a spoon in the bowl. She helped Riley balance the three dishes.

Before she walked away, she gave Riley an elbow to the side and said, "When it comes to pie and men, bigger is always better."

Meg went back to Luke's table, and Riley struggled to get the three plates to Doc's table without spilling anything.

"Here you go." She set the pie and ice cream on the table

and noticed their coffee was low. "You want more coffee with that?"

Doc looked up at her. "I think you're going to make it after all. Wasn't so sure at first, because a mute never makes a good waitress."

"Was that a yes, then?"

Doc shook his head. "One half-sass, and one half-sweet. Yep, you'll fit right in."

Riley found the coffee pots behind the counter and made the rounds filling up whatever cups she could. She skipped Luke's table altogether until he raised his cup.

"Riley, I'd like a refill too if it's not too much trouble."

She plastered on the smile she showed the world and walked over. "No problem at all, Mr. Mosier." She tipped the pot up and filled his mug.

"It's Luke."

She kept that smile on her face and the pot firmly in her hand. "Right. Do you need anything else, Mr. Mosier?"

Luke looked up at Meg then back to Riley. "Can we talk about last night?"

Meg's bright red lips puckered into a scowl. "Last night?" Her fists went to her hips. "You were with him last night?"

By the tone of her voice, Riley knew she had the wrong idea.

"No." She shook her head. "I was at a bonfire he also happened to be at."

Meg stomped her foot. "Why doesn't anyone tell me about these gatherings?"

Riley shrugged. "You didn't miss anything. Hot fire, warm beer, cold men." She turned around and walked away.

The rest of her shift was spent figuring out her way around the restaurant while Meg flirted with every man who came in.

While Meg didn't wait on a single table the rest of the night, she was quick to slide the tips into her pocket. When they turned the sign to closed, Meg handed her half and told her the other half was her training fee. Riley pocketed her thirty-two dollars and considered herself lucky she'd gotten anything at all.

CHAPTER EIGHT

Luke sat at his desk, filling out the report for his latest call. Mrs. Brown's cat had to be rescued from the roof again. The truth was, the poor cat should be rescued from Mrs. Brown. She used to call the sheriff's station because she had a soft spot for Deputy Bancroft, but now that he was married to Poppy, she didn't bother with him. She dialed the fire station directly and asked for Luke. Generally, the cat was sunning himself outside the left dormer, and as cats do, he ignored his owner and didn't come in when she called. Today though, Tom truly needed rescuing on two fronts. She'd dressed the already cantankerous cat in a clown costume, complete with a polka dotted hat and fluffy, fuzz-ball embellished collar. When Luke climbed onto the roof, he could see the resignation in the cat's eyes. Had the cat had enough and decided to hang himself from the sharp edge of the dormer window, or had the collar simply caught on a nail as he slinked by? Something told Luke it was the former. Poor Tom had that kill-me-now look in his angry piss-yellow eyes.

He finished the report and put it in the ever-increasing file dedicated to Mrs. Brown. The smell of something savory wafted through the air. He lifted his nose to inhale. Chili, if he was correct. No doubt Thomas was making his special chili with cheese omelet. Luke's stomach growled in protest for skipping his morning visit to Maisey's Diner.

Luke hadn't seen Riley for two days. He stayed out of the diner, hoping to avoid Meg, but avoiding Meg meant he had to avoid Riley. Something about her pulled at him. He wanted to dislike her, but he couldn't. He had a level of respect for someone who left everything they knew to move to another state to start fresh.

Was she running from something or running to something?

He thought about Dalton's comment that she was like everyone else, simply trying to find a place to belong. That was precisely what drove him to move to Aspen Cove.

He'd grown up in a small-town environment, working on a ranch, then moved to the city to pursue a career in firefighting. The problem was while he loved his job in Denver, he never got the sense of community he did by living in a small town. When the posting went up for the fire chief job, he'd jumped on it despite his fellow team members telling him it was a suicide mission. He'd heard it all, from how private funding would run out to how hick towns had nothing to offer. Those scare tactics were unproven and untrue. In truth, he made a higher salary here than he did in the station in

Denver. Aspen Cove was free of the office politics that came naturally with anything run by the city. Here, everyone had a job to do, and they did it well and were compensated fairly—more than fairly. As for small town offerings? Thoughts of Riley made him smile. *Things were looking up.*

He walked into the kitchen from his office to find Thomas flipping a giant omelet in a pan.

"That's big enough to feed the crew." Luke leaned in and looked at the cheese oozing from the sides of the omelet.

"No, it's big enough to feed me." Thomas touched his T-shirt-covered stomach.

They worked out together, and while Luke was in good shape, he'd have to become a gym rat to get the kind of muscle definition Thomas got by simply breathing. The man consumed a six-egg omelet each morning. The rest of his meals consisted mostly of chicken, broccoli and brown rice. Throw in a beer or two, and he was happy.

"I don't know how you do it."

Thomas slid his meal onto a plate and walked over to the table.

Luke grabbed a muffin from the daily box and took a seat across from his friend.

"I don't eat muffins, and I barely visit the diner, which happens to be your second home."

"Not true. I hang out at Bishop's Brewhouse, too."

Thomas forked a bite and pulled it to his mouth, a thread of cheese stretching all the way from the plate to his lips.

"Why are you avoiding Maisey's? Is it because of the newbie?"

Luke frowned. "No." He took a bite of his carrot cake muffin. Mondays were his favorite muffin, followed by Friday, which was always raspberry. He had to get there early on Fridays, because those were Sheriff Cooper's favorite, too. "I'm trying to get healthier."

Thomas eyed the muffin and shook his head. "Eating a muffin?"

Luke pulled the paper cup down and plucked a raisin from the side. "What? It's got carrots. I'm certain there's some kind of grain in here. Butter is dairy. The nuts have to provide something good, too."

"Keep lying to yourself about the health of muffins and the reason you're avoiding the diner." He rose, got a plate from the cabinet, a fork from the drawer and came back to the table. He sectioned half of the omelet and lifted it to the other plate, sliding it to Luke. "Eat this. At least it's full of protein."

"That almost sounds like you care."

He shook his head. "As the next in charge, I only care as far as the paperwork I'd have to fill out if you died. How would I explain a death by muffin?"

They both shared a chuckle.

"Speaking of paperwork, I finished mine for the call to Mrs. Brown's house."

"How did you explain the cat in the clown costume?"

The bite Luke took burned his tongue, so he opened his mouth and breathed around the food until he could safely chew and swallow without blistering his tongue.

"I put it down as attempted suicide."

Thomas choked on his food. "You didn't."

57

Luke nodded. "Would there be another reason to hang yourself from a dormer nail? I'd have noosed myself up long ago if I had to live with Mrs. Brown."

"Speaking of women, have you kissed and made up with Dalton's cousin?"

"No, why would I? I may have chosen my words poorly, but I still stand behind my reasoning for using them. Only an id..." He took a deep breath. "A person who lacked common sense would travel with full tanks."

"She said they were purged."

Luke rolled his eyes. "Yeah, and Mrs. Brown says Tom loves his costumes." He scraped the last of the melted cheese from the plate and ate it. "I'll apologize when I see the tags."

Thomas's eyes grew wide. His shoulders shook as a small chuckle turned into a full body, bend over, grab your stomach kind of laugh.

"What the hell's your problem?"

His friend shook his head. "You better start formulating your apology."

Thomas stood, tossed his plate into the sink, and made a quick escape toward the doorway. "Yell if you need me. Think before you speak."

The smell of citrus filled the air. Right then, the hairs stood up on the back of Luke's neck. He knew if he turned, he'd be facing Miss Blue Eyes.

"Excuse me?"

Luke slid from his chair and turned at the pace of a snail to face her.

He nodded his head. "Riley." The omelet he'd devoured

threatened to rise to his throat. He swallowed again, forcing it back down. Why this woman unsettled him so made no sense.

She stood in the doorway with one hand filled with purge tags and the other holding a muffin.

"Mr. Mosier." She took a bold step. The action spoke of confidence, but her face held a look of uncertainty. "Being new in town, it's important to me to make sure you don't have the wrong impression of me." She looked down at the tags in her hand. "I can assure you I always put safety first." She pushed the hand holding the tags toward him.

He took two steps until he stood directly in front of her. The tags tickled the edge of his fingers until he took them and looked at them. They were indeed, recent purge tags from oxygen and acetylene tanks.

She offered him the muffin. "I brought this for you, too. The tags are to prove I'm not an idiot. The muffin is a gift. Eat it, and maybe you'll be sweeter."

She pivoted around and left.

Luke stood there with his mouth hinged open.

"That one is a firecracker," Thomas said. He'd obviously been listening to the whole conversation. Could he call it a conversation? He'd said one word to her. He'd called her name before he became mute.

Luke leaned forward to make sure she was out of earshot.

"That one is trouble." He tossed the tags into the trash and took a bite of his muffin. Something about it coming from Riley made it taste sweeter. It wasn't meant as a gift at all, but a lesson. She could have stayed away and avoided him, but she didn't, and that meant something.

He wasn't sure what that something was, but he was game to find out.

"Are you going to go after her and give her back what she dished out?"

"If I chased her to give her a piece of my mind, I'd never be able to match wits with you."

Luke wanted to go after her for sure, but he wasn't sure if it was to give her a piece of his mind or pull her to him and kiss the vinegar out of her.

"You lost the wits battle long ago, my friend." He plucked the muffin from Luke's hand and tossed it into a nearby trash can. "That shit is killing your brain cells."

Thomas moved into the garage and pulled some equipment off the truck. It was time to take inventory.

While they counted hoses and axes and various other equipment, Luke thought about taking inventory of his life, too. Now that he knew Riley wasn't a temporary resident, he pondered the possibility they could become friends, possibly more.

He let out a chuckle.

"What are you laughing at?" Thomas tossed him a box of gloves. "These need to be matched and mated."

Luke laughed harder. "Maybe I'm like these gloves."

Thomas stopped and stared at the box sitting at Luke's feet. "Maybe you are. Somehow, they find themselves lost and alone, but they'd be better in pairs."

Luke stared out the open garage door down the street

toward the diner. "Funny how we can sabotage our lives with simple words." He nodded toward the street. "I called her an idiot, and she showed up and proved the idiot was me."

He dropped to his knees and began to match the misfits. Maybe that's what he loved so much about this town. It was a bunch of misfits that came together and seemed to fit well.

He liked Riley Black. When he looked at her, he saw a woman like Tom the cat. She could wear a fake smile or try on a cloak of courage, but those were simply clown costumes. At the end of the day, Riley Black was a woman on the edge of discovering who she was, and Tom was still a cat.

CHAPTER NINE

Riley's car choked out a few gasps after she killed the engine. She started to think of her Jeep as a living entity—an old lady who would say she had a sore throat and cough for effect. It was a silly thought, but one that made her smile.

She palmed the dashboard lovingly. "Thank you for always getting me where I need to go. I swear as soon as I can, I'll get you a check-up."

She saw movement to her right and stepped out of her SUV to meet Dalton halfway.

"You found the place." He walked in front of her, leading her to a door at the rear of the building.

She had to jog to keep up with his long strides. "In a hurry?" She was winded by the time she caught up with him.

"Sorry, it's a habit. Sam is always telling me to slow down. Sometimes I throw her over my shoulder so she can keep up."

He unlocked the large metal door and walked inside. The air smelled like creativity. As she breathed in, she caught hints of paint and linseed oil. There was a distinctive scent of chemicals and freshly cut wood.

They wormed their way through an industrial looking hallway, only to come out in the gallery that currently had pictures hanging everywhere.

"This is Poppy Dawson's work." He shook his head. "I mean Poppy Bancroft. You haven't met them because they're newlyweds, but he's the deputy sheriff and she's a local photographer who also works at the sheriff's office. Her father owns the Big D Ranch."

Riley's head snapped back in surprise. "Really? They call it the Big D?"

"Yep, and he takes a lot of shit for it. However, I think he likes it. Certainly better than the Little D."

Riley laughed. "They say size doesn't matter."

Dalton walked farther into the gallery. "Whoever they are, they lie."

Riley walked between the photos and recognized many of the people as residents of Aspen Cove. "She's good."

"You'll like her. She's good people. She'll be photographing the fireman calendar this year."

Riley laughed. "There's a fireman calendar?"

He nodded. "Fundraiser for the fire station." He weaved through the displays to the other side of the gallery. "Beyond this door is Sam's recording studio." He pointed down a corridor that ended in darkness. "My culinary school in on the other side." He spun around and walked back through the gallery to the wide hallway that opened up into smaller rooms. They peeked into open doors for Riley to see what the creators of Aspen Cove were up to.

"This space belongs to a woman who comes up on the weekends. She lives in Denver. I think her name is Sosie, but I'm not sure."

"Who is in charge of renting the studios?"

"That would be Deanna, Samantha's assistant."

"Does she live here?"

"Not yet, but she will. Right now, there aren't enough livable homes. Wes is flipping them as fast as he and the Lockhart brothers can, but with the growth we've got, it's not fast enough."

They walked to the next studio, and Riley peeked inside to see the floors littered with wood shavings. On a shelf were tiny whittled ornaments. Against the wall were large, ornately carved panels that resembled headboards, but she couldn't be sure.

"This is Cannon's space. He loves to work with wood." They stepped out and went to the last room on the left. The one that would share a wall with Cannon. "This is your space."

Riley stepped into the room that had beautifully stained cement floors and walls more suited for art than the tools she'd hang from them.

"This is too nice for what I do." She spun around the large open space. "Isn't there a corner of a garage or a warehouse I can use?"

Dalton went to the windows and yanked open the blinds. In the distance, she could see the top of Long's Peak. The forest wound its way down for miles and came to a stop behind the gallery.

"This is your space. Don't you like it?"

She took in the beauty of everything from the overhead lighting to the taupe colored walls.

"I love it. I'm not used to working in such a nice place. I'm not sure it has the exhaust system and fire protective features I'll need."

"You planning on burning the place down?"

"Lord, no. God, that would be awful. I'm asking because I work with fire and high heat."

He pointed to the sprinklers in the ceiling. "This has state-of-the-art safety features. Each space has its own system; that way, if something happens in one studio that requires the sprinkler system to engage, it doesn't ruin everyone else's work."

That was genius. "That's amazing."

"It is, but we'd rather it not get used."

"I'm the safest tenant you'll ever have." She walked around the room, mentally placing her equipment. "Do you remember the story of me burning my dad's workshop down?"

Dalton leaned against the wall. "I don't think I got the full version. Tell me."

She leaned against the wall and slid down to sit on the slick concrete. Dalton followed her to the floor.

She pulled the hem of her T-shirt forward and picked at the frayed edge.

"Dad was working on some kind of rack. It was a metal grid that had about twenty crosshatched sections of metal." She shook her head. "Something for Kathy to hang her pots and pans on." She pulled a thread that unraveled inches of hem. "Anyway, I'd come up behind him because Kathy said it was time to eat. I startled him, and he dropped the torch. It landed on a tarp that caught fire. We both raced toward the flames to stomp them out, but Dad pushed me aside. I tumbled back into the grid."

"Oh shit, was it still hot?" Dalton leaned forward as if she was telling him about a movie.

Talking about it made her scars ache. "Hot enough to burn through my clothes." She tried to make light of it. "If you've got a pen, we can play tick-tack-toe. There's a perfect grid of nine on my back."

"Oh God, Riley. That's awful. I bet Uncle Mike felt terrible."

She nodded. "Blamed himself until the day he died. Turns out he was drinking that day and he'd kicked over a bottle of alcohol. That's why the tarp went up in flames."

"It was his fault."

She stretched out her legs and leaned back on her hands. "Not really, it was a comedy of errors. Kathy wanted him in. I startled him. He was drunk. The torch slipped. The whole place went up in flames. After, I learned all about welding safety."

"I'm surprised you'd want to go anywhere near a welder."

"I question that myself, but it's kind of like that saying about falling off a horse and getting back on to ride again. Besides, it was the only place I could spend time with my dad."

"I bet Kathy felt terrible."

Riley nearly choked. "Are we talking about the same Kathy?" Her throat constricted, and a growl escaped. "The only time that woman would feel anything for me is if I were dead, then she'd rejoice. She hated me from the beginning because my dad loved me."

"Yeah, she wasn't all that nice. What was it about our parents that had them choosing awful spouses?"

"Even awful is kind. Your dad was an asshole, my birth mother spent less than a month with her twins before she ghosted. I found out about five years ago she died in a car accident. Couldn't even bring myself to feel anything because I didn't know her. Dad cried when I told him, though."

"Your dad had heart. No backbone, but he had heart." Dalton shook his head. "Did you heal?"

She thought about that for a minute. "No." She pushed to her feet and walked to the window. "The burns took months to heal, but those aren't the scars I carry. It's Kathy's words that echo in my head. 'You're not pretty enough, talented enough, enough of anything. Now you're damaged. What man wants to look at that for the rest of his life?'"

Dalton stood and came over to give Riley a hug. "Looks like my father wasn't the biggest asshole in the family. How about we get you moved in?"

67

Riley nodded. A trip down Memory Lane was the last place she wanted to travel.

They unloaded her Jeep. Dalton told her to leave the tanks outside the building.

"They're safe," she told him. "I did have them purged in case you heard the rumor floating around about what an idiot I am."

"There's a rumor?" He carried the biggest of her two welders inside. It was a good thing Kathy didn't know what they were worth, or she would have never let Riley have them.

"Haven't heard it, but is that why you're not a fan of Luke's? He's a safety freak."

She rolled the smaller welder on a handcart she found near the back door. "Yep, he called me out at the bonfire. I took him my tags today to prove a point. You think he'll get on a loudspeaker and make a public apology?"

"We don't have a public broadcasting system, but he's a good guy. I'm sure he'll make it up to you."

Once they brought in her metal scraps and tools, they looked around the mostly empty space.

"Thanks for this."

Dalton gave her the Black family smile. One that carried a hint of mischief. "You may not thank me after all." He moved to the door as if he needed a quick escape. "The tanks will be traded for full ones tomorrow. City Gas is coming by in the morning."

Riley felt the tears collect in her eyes. She thought she'd

have to wait a while to get to work. "You didn't have to do that."

Dalton put a hand on each side of the door and leaned forward. "But I did because Sam told me to. Like I said, you might not be grateful later."

She took a step toward him, and he took a step back. "Why is that?"

"We have an ulterior motive for setting you up, but you'll have to come to Bishop's Brewhouse tonight so Sam can fill you in."

She wanted to tell him she wasn't a barfly kind of girl, but how could she refuse to go when they'd made it possible for her to come to Aspen Cove? She wasn't homeless, jobless, or starving because of Sam, Dalton and Aunt Maisey. If they needed something from her, she'd do what it took to make it happen.

"See you then." Dalton pushed off the frame and disappeared down the dark corridor. "Shut the door behind you when you leave."

She yelled after him, "Will I get a key?"

He walked back until his silhouette was visible. "You don't need one. There's no crime here to speak of, but the doors will lock behind you. Punch in 3315 on the keypad near the door. If you ever forget the code, the door near Sam's studio hasn't locked in months. We're waiting for the electrician to order the part. See you at the Brewhouse. We'll be there by seven." He turned to walk away but stopped. "Almost forgot. There's a warehouse of shelving and workbenches in the back. It's across from the exit. Help yourself."

Riley tailed him toward the exit, but he was too fast to catch. When she got to the warehouse, her heart sang hallelujah. They had everything she could wish for.

As she dragged what she needed to her space, she thought about Luke Mosier. He was everything she didn't need, but he was something she might want.

CHAPTER TEN

Dripping with water, Luke exited the shower and grabbed a towel. The bar fell to the floor. "Damn rental." It seemed each time he fixed something, another thing broke.

Like most of the homes in Aspen Cove, his house was one inspection away from condemned, but at least the roof didn't leak, and the water ran clear, unlike many of the turn of the century homes with original plumbing. There were even a few houses that still had a well with a spigot out back.

He set the bar on the back of the toilet and wrapped the towel around his waist. It was time he made more solid plans for himself. He'd been in Aspen Cove for a while now. He knew he wanted to stay, so it made sense to find permanent lodging.

He thought of the lot between Dalton's and Cannon's houses. That would be a sweet spot. He could picture living there. Raising a family. Teaching his sons and daughters how to fish. Those thoughts brought visions of his future wife. A week ago, his mind would have drawn a blank, but today he pictured a beautiful blonde who filled out a pair of jeans perfectly.

The towel around his waist tented, and he shook his head.

"Let it go." He squirted shaving cream on his hand and rubbed it over his whiskers. "I can't let it go."

This was only one problem with living by himself. He often held full conversations as if he were two people. The other was, when he cooked, he made enough to feed a family, which meant he generally ate the same thing all week.

He shaved, dressed and grabbed his guitar. Tuesdays were open mic night at Bishop's Brewhouse. Hopefully, Dalton would be there, and he could inquire about the lot. At thirty-four, Luke needed to think of his future.

The weather was warm, and the walk to the Brewhouse cleared his head. He turned the corner to Main Street and saw the rig from the station backing into the garage.

Luke sprinted toward the station with his guitar strapped to his back.

Thomas hopped down from the driver's seat. He tugged off his heavy yellow jacket and tossed it toward James. "Hang it for me, will ya?"

"What happened? I didn't get a call." Luke pulled his guitar from his back and set it against the wall.

"Abby happened." Thomas scrubbed his eyes with his palms.

"Another small kitchen fire?"

Thomas shut the rig door and walked toward the break room.

"Man, I swear when we showed up, she was fanning the flames. Either she's the worst cook ever or she's setting them on purpose to get us to her place."

Luke laughed. "She's got a thing for you." Abby Garrett never had a fire in her life until Thomas Cross moved into town. If anything was burning at Abby's house, it was her passion for Luke's second-in-command.

He opened the fridge and pulled out two sodas, offering one up to Luke.

"No, thanks. I'm heading off to Bishop's for a beer. You want to join me?"

Thomas popped his soda top and looked around the station. "I'm on call all night, but I might stop by for a soda."

"You should take her out. She's a nice woman." He walked over and unplugged the toaster. It was a habit he had since he heard about an old toaster igniting from a bad cord in the middle of the night.

"Nah, man. While she might be nice and easy on the eyes, she's not my type. She spends her days with insects. What the hell would we talk about?"

Luke grinned. Ever since he'd met Abby, he'd memorized an arsenal of bee jokes but hadn't found an opportunity to use them.

"You can talk about music."

Thomas shrugged. "She's probably a country junkie."

"Doubt it." He looked to the ceiling like he was thinking,

then gave Thomas an I've-got-it look. "I'd bet her favorite singer is Sting and her favorite group is the Bee Gees."

"You're such an ass. No wonder you're single, too."

"I'm single because I haven't found the right one, but I'm looking." He leaned against the counter. All this talk of women had him thinking about Riley.

"Got your sights set on the hottie?" Thomas kicked off the cabinet and opened the fridge where he kept containers of chicken, rice, and broccoli. He pulled one of his pre-made meals out and stuck it in the microwave.

"Are you talking about Riley?"

Thomas laughed. "The fact you know who I'm talking about proves I'm right."

"Nope. I'm about as interested in Riley as you are in bees." Luke knew Abby wasn't Thomas's type, not because she wasn't attractive or nice, but because Thomas, while being a giant of a man, was actually afraid of bees. Each time a call came in to the station for Abby, he suited up in full gear. He claimed safety as his motivation, but everyone knew better. They'd seen him run buck naked from the station once when he found a bee in the bathroom.

Luke held in a laugh. He was pretty sure Abby set that one up, too.

"You're such a liar." He leaned forward and smelled the air. "Cologne tonight?"

"I shaved. I always use aftershave."

The microwave beeped, and Thomas pulled his meal out and headed for the table. "You shave every day, and you never smell that nice."

He couldn't argue with the man. Didn't want to because he was right. Cologne wasn't something Luke wore regularly, but he spritzed some on in case there was a chance he'd see a pretty blonde at the bar.

"Be careful with that one. She plays with fire, but you might be the one to get burned. Don't forget it's her family who signs your paycheck."

"Wrong again, buddy. It's me who signs yours." Luke walked over and snatched a piece of broccoli from Thomas's plate. "I'll see you at the Brewhouse."

He picked up his guitar and headed for the bar. Tuesdays weren't crazy busy, but there was a decent crowd when he walked inside.

He scouted the place and found his heart sinking when Riley wasn't present. He wasn't sure what he liked best about her, the fact she was pretty or she was a contrast of character for him to figure out.

He spied Dalton and Samantha at a table by the window. Seeing them made him think about the sweet piece of land by the lake.

"Hey, you two, can I join you for a moment?"

Samantha pointed to one of the empty chairs. "You gonna sing me a song?"

He laughed. "Maybe I'm interviewing for a new job. Got a place for me in your band?" He set his guitar by the wall.

Dalton chimed in, "Tired of holding your hose?"

"Dude, you shouldn't be talking about my hose in front of your fiancée."

75

Dalton leaned in and whispered, "I'm not worried. She's marrying me for my kitchen skills."

Luke laughed. "I wouldn't be bragging about that, man."

"You two need to stop." Samantha put her hand gently on Dalton's arm. "Honey, you know I fell in love with you when you used your pickup line." She tapped her chin. "What was it... oh yeah: baby, if you were a fruit, you'd be a fineapple."

"He didn't."

She laughed. "No, the first time I met him, he called me a boy and accused me of being an arsonist."

"Damn brain like a steel trap, my woman." Dalton leaned over and kissed Samantha's cheek. "But she *is* an arsonist. She set my heart on fire."

Luke made a retching sound. "I'm not sure I can handle this much cheese in one day."

"You're the one who came to our table." Dalton waved him off. "Leave if you're not a fan of cheesy pick-up lines and true love."

"I'm a fan, all right, but that's not why I stopped by your table." He was never good at negotiating. Not a pro at going after what he wanted. He was more of a sideline guy and jumped on opportunities when they presented themselves, like Aspen Cove did. Going after something that wasn't already offered wasn't in his lane, but it was worth the risk.

"If you're here to ask for my cousin's hand in marriage, you'll have to get her to like you first. She's not a fan."

"Ha ha ha," Luke flatlined. "You're a real comedian tonight. I'm not after your cousin. I want something else that belongs to you."

Dalton lifted an eye. "You better start talking or running."

"Jeez, I swear sometimes I think the high altitude has frizzled everyone's brain cells." He shook his head hard enough to bruise a few of his own. "I wanted to ask about the lot next to your house. Are you going to build a McMansion on it, or would you be willing to sell it?"

Samantha sat up. "You want my lot?" She beamed from ear to ear.

"I'd like to lay down some roots, and a house on the lake seems like a great place to start."

"If I sell you my land, would you sign a contract to stay as the fire chief for life?"

"Seriously? You'd blackmail me into staying for life?"

Cannon came over and set a beer in front of Luke. "You gonna play or what?" He nodded toward the empty stage. "I'm only buying you beer if you play."

Luke loved this damn town and the people in it. He'd been there less than a year, but he felt like he'd known these people all his life. "I'll play after I negotiate my life of servitude."

Cannon pushed the beer closer, and the bubbles splashed over the rim. "I'm only asking for a song." He turned and walked away.

He looked at Samantha and Dalton, who were whispering back and forth. It was Dalton who spoke first.

"Sam got her insurance settlement. She'd been talking about rebuilding."

Luke nodded. "I get it. It would be a hard piece of land to

give up. I'll keep looking." He made to stand, but Samantha reached out and touched his arm.

"I'm not opposed to selling. I was going to rebuild the cabin and sell it anyway. Dalton and I want to keep the feel of the town the same. Wouldn't be possible if I built a McMansion, as you called it. If we need more space, we'll build up, not out."

Hope filled his heart. "You'll consider selling it?"

"I'd give it to you if you promised to stay," Samantha answered.

"I'm staying, but I'll pay fair market price."

"Deal," Sam and Dalton said in unison and picked up their glasses for a toast, which in Aspen Cove was kind of like a gentlemen's agreement. Tapping glasses was as good as shaking hands.

Luke said, "Doc can run some numbers, and we'll go from there." Doc Parker was not only one of the town's doctors, he was also the real estate agent and the officiant at all the town weddings.

Samantha turned to Dalton. "Look, honey, we came for a drink and to see Riley and ended up with a neighbor."

Luke knew the minute Riley walked into the bar. Being a male-heavy population, the presence of a new, pretty face always quieted the men. When the din was silenced, he figured it was either Riley or Big Foot. Both would mute a room, but there hadn't been a Sasquatch sighting in the Rockies for years, so he was putting his money on Riley.

He looked up to find her standing near the table. The look she gave him was all he needed to know. There wasn't an ounce of forgiveness in those big, beautiful blue eyes. He'd hoped the few days he'd put between them would allow her time to get over her anger.

He pulled his keys from his pocket and held them in front of her.

As a reminder to himself not to jump to conclusions, he'd attached one of her purge tags.

"Didn't want to forget," he said.

"Asshole," she hissed under her breath.

"Time for me to go." He palmed the neck of his guitar and picked up his beer to head to the stage.

CHAPTER ELEVEN

She dropped her frown and replaced it with a smile. "Hey, Cuz and Sam." She slid into the seat Luke had vacated. It was warm and welcoming, the opposite of the man himself.

"You get all moved in?"

"I did," she gushed. "I pulled a bunch of stuff in from the warehouse, like workbenches and shelving. Hope that's okay."

"That what it's there for. Glad you could use it." Dalton signaled to Cannon, who rushed over.

"Good to see you again, Riley. Wine or beer, or something stronger?"

"Wine." With a few dollars in her pocket from tips, she could afford a glass. "Red if you have it, white if you don't."

"Red it is." He went behind the bar and shoved the tabby cat off the register.

"Does that cat have one eye?" Riley asked.

Samantha laughed. "That's Mike, and he fits in with us misfits." The orange tabby swished by Riley's legs and crawled onto the narrow ledge of the window. "Sage's dog Otis has three legs. Charlie and Trig's dog Clovis has a thyroid issue, so he looks like a footstool."

"Then I should fit right in."

"You'll be fine here." Dalton leaned back. "You're a Black; no one is going to mess with you."

She hated to burst his bubble, but several people were messing with her already. The top two on her list were Meg and Luke.

She turned to Samantha. "Dalton said you had an ulterior motive for giving me the space at the Guild Creative Center."

Sam didn't even look at him before she slugged him in the arm. "I never said that. You could have the space no matter what, but I thought maybe a good way to get you started on your craft would be to give you a project." She looked up at Dalton. "It's a good thing he's handsome and can cook, because he'd make an awful secretary."

Looking at them warmed Riley's heart. It was nice to see true love at work.

"Tell me what you need. I'm still working on my craft, but I'm willing to try anything. I owe you."

Sam shook her head. "You don't owe us a thing. In fact, we'll pay for the supplies and your time."

"What's this project?" She knew this wasn't the time to argue about payment. There was no way she'd charge Dalton and Sam anything. They'd opened up a world of opportunities for her by giving her a space to work. That gift was priceless.

Sam leaned in. She was a tiny thing, with long, dark hair and a hundred-watt smile. "The benefits concert is called Music On Fire, and I thought it might be cool to have some pyrotechnics. Then I thought it would be cooler if I could have a piece of art that flames shot out of." She sipped her beer and bounced in her seat. "Cooler yet if it could be a guitar or something like that."

There was a tap on the microphone, and all heads turned to Luke, who took a drink of his beer and set it at his feet.

"Hey, y'all. I'm dedicating this first song to a girl. She'll know who she is." He tuned his guitar and began to play.

Riley looked around the room for the girl he was singing to, but there didn't seem to be a lot of single females in the bar. When she looked back at him, he was staring at her singing a song about his stupid mouth.

"Something going on between you two?" Sam lifted a perfectly plucked brow.

Riley let her breath out in a laugh. "No, no, no, there's absolutely nothing going on between us. He's an asshole."

"Luke?" Sam set her hand on Riley's. "Honey, you need to get out more if you think he's an asshole. Assholes beat you up or burn down your house. They don't play guitars, singing songs of apology."

Riley took one more look at Luke, who was still focused on her. "That's an I'm sorry song?"

"They don't get much better than that. What did he do that needs an apology?"

In the scheme of things, he didn't do much more than most people in her life. "He didn't give me the benefit of the doubt."

Sam shook her head like she got it. Dalton looked at her like a fish out of water. His eyes bulged, and his mouth opened and closed.

Sam turned to him and said, "This is one of those times where you'd be better off nodding and smiling."

He closed his lips and did as she said.

Luke finished his song. Riley picked up her glass and gave him a silent toast before she turned back to Sam.

"You want flaming instruments?" She opened her purse and dug around for a pen and slip of paper. When she found one, she made a quick sketch of a guitar. "Something like this, but about five feet tall?"

"Yes, is that possible?" Samantha bounced in her seat. She looked up and saw someone she knew. "Look who's here." She pointed to a group of men at the pool table. "Those are the Lockharts. Name about says it right. Hearts locked up tight. They date but don't commit."

"Are you two going to gossip about the men in the bar or talk sculptures?" Dalton was already halfway out of his seat.

"Both. Go play pool."

Dalton gave Sam a kiss before he took off toward the pool table.

"I can do the sculpture, but I'm not sure how to add the fire."

Sam looked down at the rough drawing. "What about sparklers or something like that?"

Riley saw her vision and didn't think sparklers would do it. She scribbled a few more things on the paper. "What if I put several holders on the back of the sculpture and we put something like a jackpot fountain?"

"A what?"

"It's a firework that's like a sparkler on steroids. It will shoot sparks and whistle for a good amount of time, enough to get a reaction from the crowd. The only issue is, someone would have to light them."

She looked around the room now filled to standing room only and nearly ninety percent men. "We do have some hunky firemen; but then again, I think you've already noticed."

Riley took a big gulp of her wine. "I have no idea what you're talking about."

"Of course not. Let's fill your glass up so we can toast to your new life in Aspen Cove." She held up their empty glasses, and somehow through the crowd, Cannon appeared with refills.

They clinked glasses and looked around the room. Another person had taken the stage, and when Riley scanned the room, she saw Luke by the pool table with the Lockharts and Dalton.

"It should be illegal to have all of them in the same room."

Riley ignored Sam and turned over the paper to sketch another instrument on the backside. While she tried to disregard the testosterone weighing the opposite side of the room down, she couldn't—and each time she looked, Luke was watching her.

"How detailed do you want these?"

"What's your skill set?" Sam turned the sketch to face her.

Riley's heart slammed into her chest. What would happen if she messed this project up? Sam would be giving a concert, and her fans would see Riley's work.

Part of her wanted to shut it down right away and tell her she couldn't do it, but she did owe them something, if only to try.

"I can't say what I can make is what you're looking for, but I sure as hell will try to build you something you can be proud to stand by."

Sam reached for the pen and drew lines shooting from the head of the guitar. "I was thinking if you could get the shape down, that's all I care about. We could put some of your jackpot fountains shooting left and right. Try to keep the sparks contained to the stage. I thought about having one, but what about two? One for each side of the stage, then Luke and Thomas can light them up for the finale."

"Okay." Riley's hands shook as she folded the sketch in half and shoved it and the pen back into her purse. "When do you need them? Did I hear three weeks?"

Sam made the perfect shocked emoji face, with her eyes squinted shut and her teeth showing in a broad grin. "Yes. Is it possible?"

Riley took another big swig of wine and laughed. "I hear anything's possible here in Aspen Cove."

"You're catching on." Sam got up and picked up their empty glasses. "Drinks are on me. I'll bring a fresh one back."

She turned to walk away and stopped. "Oh, and I'll have whatever supplies you need delivered."

Before she could say anything else, Sam was gone and Luke was standing in front of her. "Do you need another glass of wine?"

She shook her head. "No, Sam's bringing me a refill."

"Great." He shifted on his heels. "I am sorry, Riley. It's that—"

"I get it. You don't have to apologize anymore. It's all good."

He leaned over. He was so close she could smell his minty breath. "Is it all good?"

After two glasses of wine, it was definitely good. Good thing she lived within walking distance, because she could stumble back to her apartment.

A shadow fell over the table, and a large man with dark hair and blue eyes patted Luke on the back.

"Are you going to introduce me?"

Luke stood up. He went head to head with the handsome man, but Luke wasn't nearly as wide.

"No, Noah. Go back to Cross Creek and find your own girl."

Noah pulled out a chair and sat beside Riley. "We don't make them this lovely in Cross Creek." He offered his hand. "I'm Noah Lockhart."

She took his hand and was surprised hers nearly disappeared in his palm. "Riley Black."

His brows shot up. "Dalton's sister?"

"No." She shook her head, and her hair tumbled around her shoulders. "I'm his cousin."

"She's a welder," Luke added.

Riley wasn't sure if he thought that was cool or if he mentioned it to turn Mr. Tall, Dark, and Handsome off. Not many women picked up a welding gun and went to work.

"Welding? That's awesome. Maybe we can call you if we need some work done." Luke moved beside Riley and crossed his arms over his chest like he was a standing sentry. "My brothers and I own Lockhart Construction. We refurbed the Guild Creative Center."

"Beautiful building. I've got a studio there."

"You're an artist?"

To say so felt like a lie. Didn't she have to sell something to be legit? "I'm working on it."

"You know the saying, 'The harder I work, the luckier I get.' Who taught you to weld?"

"My father, but he passed this year. I'm carrying on the legacy."

"Why welding? It's a bit out of the norm."

Riley giggled. She looked up at Luke for a moment. "What I like the most is the way I can take something hard and rigid and make it bend to my will."

CHAPTER TWELVE

Bend to her will? Luke didn't take Riley to be the alpha female type—but then again, he hadn't considered much about her beyond her fabulous curvy figure and her pretty face.

He leaned against the window, dropping his hands to his sides.

Mike, in an uncharacteristically friendly gesture, moved under Luke's fingers for a pet.

Riley looked at the cat, then up to Luke. "Looks like you made a friend." She reached over and traced her fingers up Mike's back until her fingers touched his and a tingle raced up his spine. "They say animals are good judges of character."

She smiled wide, and he swore the entire bar lit up.

"Is that right?"

She shrugged. "That's what I hear. Then again, Mike only has one eye, so maybe he's off his game."

Across the room, Dalton called for Noah.

"Looks like I'm being paged." He set his hand on hers. "Save a dance for me for later?"

She looked at Noah like he hung the moon. "You bet. All we need now is music." Her eyes traveled up to Luke. "Are you going to entertain us again?"

Noah rose, and Luke took his seat. "In a bit. I was hoping you'd entertain me first."

Noah walked away, leaving the two of them alone at the table.

"He has a reputation as a player," Luke said.

"Does he?"

He nodded. While he'd never actually seen Noah be anything but respectful, he'd never seen him with the same woman twice. "He's not a forever kind of guy." He didn't know why that slipped out. "If that's what you're looking for."

Riley moved to the side so she could watch Noah walk to the table. He said hello to a few people he passed, then took up his pool cue.

"I'm not looking for anything, but he seems okay. Besides, it seems to me everyone has a reputation at some point." She looked around the room.

Luke followed her line of sight and noticed Meg sitting at the bar scowling at him, so he turned to focus on Riley.

"Do I?"

She laughed. "With others, or with me?"

He leaned back in the chair and tried to relax, but he could feel Meg's daggers.

"It's your story, you fill in the blanks." He knew he had a

reputation, but he considered being responsible and on top of safety in the small town a good thing.

"I've only heard good things about you."

She said it like it was a lie that stung her tongue.

"But your experience is different because I was trying to uphold my original reputation?"

"The jury is still out as far as my opinion goes. Your apology went a long way to healing the wounds to my fragile ego."

"Fragile? This word coming from a girl who likes to bend things to her will?"

She let out a deep breath. "As with everything, there's the dream and the reality. I fear I've been the one to bend all my life. I'm like a young sapling always trying to weather the storm."

There was a hint of sadness in her voice that made him want to pull her into his arms and hold her.

"I'm sorry about your father." He considered his family and knew how difficult it would be to lose his father, brother or sister. While they might not live in close proximity, they stayed in touch. He was in the process of convincing his father to move to Aspen Cove. Lloyd Dawson was looking for some help on his ranch, and while his father was happy in Wyoming, Luke knew he could be happy here, too.

She turned her almost empty wine glass around and around. The blood-red liquid left splashed up the sides and beaded down to pool at the bottom.

"I miss him. He was a troubled man, but he was a good

man." She picked up her glass and finished it off. "I should probably get going."

Without a thought, he laid his hand on hers. "Stay." He looked over his shoulder to see Noah break for the next game of pool. He didn't want to set Riley up with him, but he'd use the man to keep her here. "Besides, you promised a dance to Noah."

Her eyes grew wide. "You want me to dance with Noah?"

He shook his head. "Nope, but I don't want you to go either. I'd like a chance to repair your opinion of me."

"I don't have an opinion of you anymore. I thought you were an asshole, but I think I was wrong."

He rose from the table. "Now that I have a clean slate, let me buy you a drink, and I'll endeavor to create a better first impression."

She laughed. The sound was like a song that filled the air. "You can't have a second first impression."

"Nope, but you can have a first second impression. Let's hope I do better this time around."

She slid her glass toward him. "Thanks for hanging out with me." She looked past him and waved to someone at the bar.

When he turned around, he saw Meg slide off the barstool and walk toward them. "Watch that one," he warned.

She plastered a smile on her face. "Oh, I will. My father shared his wisdom before he died." She glanced at the approaching Meg. "Keep your friends close, and your enemies closer."

"Which is she?" he asked.

"Probably someone I should keep closer."

He leaned in so close, he could smell the citrus scent of her shampoo. "Which am I?"

"The jury is still out."

He straightened up. "I'll send a glass of wine over right away." He waved to Cannon at the bar and pointed to Riley, then held a finger in the air. "The next song is for you."

"Hey, handsome." Meg sidled up to him, putting her hand on his lower back and tucking her thumb in the belt loop of his pants. "My drink is almost empty, too."

Luke looked at Meg. "You're right. I'll have Cannon send you over a water."

Her eyes narrowed, and her lips pursed.

"How come I only get a water?"

He moved to the side, so she'd have to let him loose. "Because you're driving, and cars and alcohol don't make great friends."

"Aww, you care."

"Sure, I care enough to protect everyone from stupidity, and driving while under the influence is stupid."

"That's as bad as driving with full tanks of flammable gas," Riley added.

Luke turned so Meg couldn't see him. "Almost." He took a step toward the stage. "Don't forget what your father told you."

Cannon showed up with a glass of wine for Riley. He turned around and said, "Meg wants a glass of tap water. Put it on my tab."

Inside, he laughed all the way to the stage. It wasn't that

he disliked Meg; he didn't like her. There was a difference. One thing was certain: he didn't trust her. She was sugary sweet on the outside, but something told him she was bitter on the inside.

On the other hand, Riley was trying to be salty on the outside, but her sweetness came shining through.

He climbed up on stage and tapped the mic.

"This one is for all those people who are rigid and hard."

About eighty percent of the men in the bar hooted and howled.

Luke chuckled. "Yeah, wasn't going there. This song is about learning to bend."

He sang a country song about trust, love, and forgiveness. The whole time, he kept his eyes locked to Riley's, who never once took her eyes off him. Something had changed in their dynamic, and all it took was a minute of time, an apology and a song. Throw in a glass of wine, and he was well on his way to a new reputation.

He strummed a few tunes until he played an upbeat song that got several people moving on the small dance floor.

Noah left the game he'd lost and strolled over to Riley. He couldn't hear the conversation but saw her rise and offer him her hand.

Luke didn't care to watch them dance. It made his stomach clench and ache when Noah moved her around the dance floor to the beat of the music.

Someone called out for a slower song, but he'd be damned if he'd play something that put Riley into Noah's arms. When he finished the song, he set his guitar against the wall and made his way to Riley's table.

"They make a cute couple, don't they?" Meg asked. She scooted her chair closer to the one he took.

"They're not a couple. They recently met."

Meg frowned, then replaced the dour look with a smile. "They could be. We could be."

"Look Meg, I'm not looking for anyone or anything."

She leaned in and set her head on his shoulder. "I'm not just anyone, Luke, and I'm certainly something, but you'll never know unless you try."

"That was fun." Riley came back all smiles and bright eyes. "I haven't danced in years."

Noah looked over his shoulder toward his brothers, who were standing by the door, looking impatient to leave.

"Thanks for the dance, beautiful. I'll stop by the diner to see you."

"That sounds great. See you then." She flopped into her chair and took a long drink of wine.

"I can't believe Noah Lockhart danced with you."

Riley wiped the sweat from her brow. "Why is that?"

Meg shrugged. "I don't know. You don't seem his type."

Luke separated himself from her. "He has a type?"

Meg laughed. "Probably not, but you seem more of a forever girl, and the Lockharts... they don't seem your type."

Luke moved so he was equidistant between Meg and Riley. "Do you have a type, Riley?"

She rested her elbows on the table and her head on her

94

hands. "I do. My prerequisites include honesty, kindness, compassion."

Meg rolled her eyes. "Boring. What you need is exciting, good in bed and has a job." She took her lipstick from her purse and slicked on another coat of pin-up girl red. "Take Luke here, for instance." She scooted her chair so they were side by side again. "He's a fireman, so I would deduce he likes his women hot with a lot of sizzle."

"You want another wine?" He lifted from his seat and walked to the bar without waiting for an answer. Riley was a bit tipsy, but she wasn't drunk, and he'd make sure she got home okay.

"Are you doubling up tonight?" Cannon asked when Luke got to the bar. His eyes went to the table where the two women sat.

"Oh hell, man, I can't get rid of one."

"Which one do you want to ditch?"

"I'll take a glass of red and an exit strategy. Can you tie Meg down while I run?"

Cannon poured the wine and flagged over a guy from the pool table. He whispered in his ear and waited for the guy to disappear. "I got you covered. Give it five minutes."

Luke walked back with Riley's wine. "Here you go."

"Thank you."

He sat opposite Meg, trying to put more distance between them.

"Empty-handed again. You only have wine for the new girl?"

Luke ignored her. "What did I miss?"

Riley giggled and then laughed. "I think Meg has a plan for world domination."

"No, but now you have the eye of the two sexiest men in town, I'm going to have to find you cement boots and a nice place in the lake." She laughed until the guy from the pool table appeared.

He looked between the two women. His eyes stayed on Riley for a moment too long, but then he turned to Meg. "Hey, beautiful. I need a good luck charm. Want to hold my stick?"

Meg turned back to Riley. "Finally, a man who knows what he wants." She offered the guy her hand as she stood. "I'll be back." She walked with an exaggerated sway of her hips to the pool table.

"I'm not sure if she wants to braid my hair or yank it out."

"I'm not sure she's sure either. Where were we?"

"I don't know where you were, but I was going to call it a night. I've got work in the morning, and Meg yields a mean whip as a taskmaster." She took a few drinks of her wine and set it down. "I hate to waste this, but I'm afraid if I finish it, I won't be able to walk home."

He looked down at the half-full glass of wine, picked it up and emptied it. "There, no waste."

"Thank you." She rose from her chair and grabbed the table for balance.

"You okay?"

She removed her fingers from the edge of the table one at a time, as if letting go all at once would be too risky.

When she was standing on her own two feet, she smiled

and said, "I got this." She swayed to the front door and turned around to grace him with a smile.

Not wanting Meg to see him leave with her, he raced toward the back door of the bar. He passed Cannon on his way. "Thanks, man."

"You don't need to thank me. You're picking up that guy's tab for the rest of the night."

Something told Luke it would be worth every cent.

He ran around the building and caught up with Riley in front of the bakery. She was making her way around the block.

"Hey, you." He wanted to make his presence known so he didn't frighten her.

She pressed her hand to her chest and gasped. "Oh my God. You scared the living daylights out of me."

"I said something before I approached."

"You did. I'm sorry. I... I wasn't expecting you."

He lifted a brow. "Were you expecting someone else?"

She staggered to the side and pressed her hand against the brick building. "No, I wasn't expecting anyone, but you're a pleasant surprise."

Warmth flooded his insides. "So were you when you showed up in Aspen Cove."

She licked her lips. "You sure about that? I was under the impression I was a problem, given the fact I'm so stupid, stupid, stupid."

"Will you ever forgive me for that?" He wrapped his arm around her shoulder and led her toward the back entrance to the bakery and the door he knew led to her apartment.

"I may, but shouldn't a girl milk it for all it's worth?"

He stopped in front of her door. She leaned against it, and he bracketed her body with his hands against the door.

"Somehow, you don't seem the type."

"That's right, we all have types. Yours is hot, with sizzle." She hung on to the 'z' sound, which made the word itself hot.

He leaned in until he was a breath away from her lips. "I don't have a type, but if I did, she'd be you." He pressed his lips tentatively to hers. Any lack of interest, and he'd pull away. That's not what happened.

Riley's hands wrapped around him. One behind his back, and the other behind his head. She moaned, and the littlest separation of her lips gave him the opening he needed to deepen the kiss.

One stroke of his tongue, and she was pulling him close. Her softness molded into the hard planes of his body.

Their tongues moved against each other. She tasted like wine and something sweet like candy.

His hands threaded through her hair, and he pulled her closer. He'd climb inside her if he could but pinned against the back door of the bakery wasn't where he thought he'd make his move. Hell, he wasn't prepared for any kind of move. All he knew was, kissing Riley Black was like seeing color for the first time.

On the next moan she made, he pulled away. *Keep them wanting more,* his father always said.

"I should let you go. You have an early morning."

She licked the moisture from her lips. Even under the

light of the moon, he could see a blush rise to her cheeks. He wasn't sure if he saw embarrassment or regret.

"Don't overthink it. It was a kiss." He stepped back. "A hot, sizzling, damn good kiss."

She smiled, then turned around to unlock her door.

He waited until she was inside before he walked away. Oh, how he didn't want to walk away.

CHAPTER THIRTEEN

Shit, shit, shit! Riley used a bar towel to flag away the smoke from the toaster.

"Burned it again?" Meg walked by, and with the tips of her fingers, she plucked the blackened bread from the toaster. "I told you to make sure it was on setting two." She pointed to the dial, which was turned to five.

"I swear I adjusted it like you said."

Meg kicked out a hip and stood in front of her like a mom ready to chastise. "Too much to drink last night?"

Riley thought about the night before. Had she kissed Luke? Or had she truly had too much wine and imagined it? "I had a few glasses, but not enough to eat away my brain cells."

She twisted the knob back to two and walked away.

She remembered everything with clarity. The way he'd

rushed to meet up with her. How chivalrous he was to walk her home, and how hot that damn kiss was.

She would have thought he'd taste like beer or whiskey, but he didn't. The kiss lingered for minutes, and when he pulled away, she was left with the taste of peppermint and a tingle that didn't leave her body until she pleasured herself to thoughts of him.

The bell above the diner door rang, and she whipped around, hoping to see Luke walk inside, but it was Thomas. He waved and sat on Riley's side of the restaurant.

She hurried over with a pot of coffee. "Good morning. Did you want coffee?"

He turned over his cup and slid it to the edge of the table. "Keep it coming, Riley. I need enough caffeine to get me through this contract." He opened the folder he carried and pulled out a thick packet of papers.

"That looks daunting."

"Decided on a house finally." He pointed to the page that had a small picture of the house. "Doc's waiving his fee as realtor because the house needs so much work. He said the money was better spent getting new pipes before winter."

"Sounds like sage advice." She took her order pad from her pocket. "You want to eat, or just coffee?"

"I'll take bacon and eggs with wheat toast and home fries."

She wanted to ask him if anyone would be joining him, namely Luke, but she didn't. Instead, she leaned over and took a peek at the house.

"Pansy Lane?" She couldn't stop the giggle.

"I know, right? But it's more square feet for the money. I almost decided against it simply because of the street name, but it has three bedrooms and two baths as opposed to the other house I was considering on Hyacinth. This place has a few years left on the roof, which will allow me to spend my money on the important stuff, like upgrading plumbing and electricity."

"Three bedrooms? Getting ready to start a family?" She knew Thomas was single. About everyone in town talked about how all the firemen were available. She'd heard a local woman named Abby was beyond smitten with Thomas.

He shook his head. "No way. I'm not interested in a wife or kids."

"But you'll have three bedrooms. What will you do with them?" She picked up the coffee pot.

"One I'll sleep in, one will be a gym, and one will be a man cave."

Riley laughed. "The whole place will be a man cave."

Just then, the door opened, the bell rang, and Doc Parker came into the diner. He looked around, and once he spotted Thomas, he headed his way.

Riley turned over the empty mug and poured him a cup. He came every day and ordered the same thing: two pancakes, a half order of bacon, a cup of coffee and a piece of pie.

"Putting your order in now, Doc." She stepped back so he could slide into the booth.

"You're a sweet one, Riley." He looked at Thomas. "She'd

make a mighty fine wife. This one here is magic. I don't even have to ask, and she knows what I want."

Riley walked off before she could hear Thomas's reply, but she could imagine it. He'd probably tell Doc he didn't have a girlfriend and wouldn't want a wife.

She slid her order slip into the wheel and spun it around so Dalton would see it. "Order up," she called.

She readied Thomas's toast, sticking two slices into the toaster and double checking to make sure it was set to two. She'd wait another five minutes before she dropped them down.

When the bell above the door rang, she didn't look. She'd nearly given herself whiplash a half-dozen times because she thought it might be Luke. This time, she ignored the customer and combined ketchup bottles. Since Doc and Thomas sat in her station, Meg would take the next guest anyway.

Next, she lined up the salt and pepper shakers and filled them to the top. Better to get her side work done throughout the day than wait until the end.

She heard the trill of Meg's fake laugh echo above the soft hum of whispered conversations, clanking silverware and hums of a satisfactory meal.

Spinning around, she found Luke at his normal table. Meg made herself at home across from him.

The double doors of the kitchen swung out, and Aunt Maisey appeared.

"Popping in to say hello." She touched her shellacked hair. "I've got an appointment with Marina. Ben is in the back if you need anything. Dalton is heading to his culinary school."

Maisey had been mostly absent lately. Riley wasn't certain if it was because the diner was covered and she was taking a long overdue break or if maybe her aunt was avoiding her. *Stop putting ideas in your head. She loves you and told you to come.*

It was hard to break old habits. Hard to stop the record of inadequacy from replaying in her head. Hard to remember she was no longer the target of her stepmother's dissatisfaction.

"Getting a trim?" She wiped down the counter in front of the toaster and tossed the damp towel into the soapy bucket on the shelf below.

Maisey touched her hair, which didn't move in strands, but as an entire unit on her head.

"I'm not sure. I've been thinking about how proud of you I am and how brave you were to take a chance and come to Aspen Cove. It's been a long time since I've stepped out of my comfort zone. The only risk I've taken lately is Ben, and he was a good bet. You've inspired me to try something new."

Joy rose from Riley's chest to bloom into a smile on her face. "Me?"

Maisey pinched her cheek. "Yes, you." She leaned in and kissed the spot that was now, no doubt, blooming red.

Bouncing on her feet, Riley clapped her hands quietly. "Come and show me right away." Riley lowered the toast, knowing her order would be up soon. She picked up the coffee pot to make her rounds and stepped across the invisible line that separated Meg's table from hers. She moved throughout the diner, refilling coffees for everyone.

"Order up," Ben called. She lifted on her tiptoes to see what was steaming in the window. An order of biscuits and gravy and a chili and cheese omelet sat there waiting for Meg.

"Your order is ready," Riley said as she stopped by the table and offered Luke a coffee.

He smiled broadly and turned his mug over. "Morning, Riley. How was your night?"

Meg snorted. "She left early and went home. How fun could that have been?" She lifted from the table. "She's more fizzle than sizzle." She looked to the order window, then looked back at Luke. "Come to think of it, you left early, too."

Riley was certain Meg's nails sharpened and grew ready to strike, but when she looked at her, all she saw was a calm smile. *Maybe I'm misjudging her. She's snarky, but she hasn't been mean.* More old damn habits she had to break. She looked down at Luke and realized she was doing the same thing to Meg that he had done to her. She was assuming the worst.

"I had business to take care of," Luke said.

Meg walked in front of Riley, forcing her to take a step back from the booth. She ran her hand up Luke's arm until it rested on his shoulder and made a hissing sound reminiscent of pork rinds crackling on an open fire. "I'll be back."

"You've got a fan," Riley said to Luke.

"More like a parasite."

She laughed until a string of expletives came from behind the front counter.

Meg was slapping the smoking toaster with a terrycloth towel. Soon, the cloth caught fire and chaos erupted.

Luke jumped from his seat. He ran behind the counter and unplugged the toaster and grabbed the flaming towel from Meg and tossed it in a nearby sink, dousing it with water.

Meg burst into tears and held her hand against her chest. "I'm injured." She turned toward Riley. "You nearly burned the place down."

"I didn't."

Meg looked at the toaster, where the dial was turned back to five. "You did that on purpose. I told you it couldn't be past two, or it would burn the toast." She yelled loud enough to grab the attention of everyone in the diner. Even Ben pushed through the swinging doors to investigate what the fuss was. "You're dangerous and irresponsible." She lowered her hand, which wasn't even red. "I'm burned."

Luke took Meg's hand in his and led her to the sink, where he turned on the cold tap. "I don't see anything, Meg."

She pouted. "Just because you don't see it doesn't mean it doesn't hurt."

Doc came around the counter to take a look. "No redness, no blister. You'll live, young lady." His eyes went to the window and then to Riley. "I may not if you don't feed me."

"Right." She jumped into action by grabbing Doc and Thomas' order from the window and rushing them to their table. "The toast will be another minute. I'm sorry."

Thomas looked up from his packet of papers, then over

his shoulder at Luke, who had returned to his booth with Meg.

"You didn't have to start a fire to get his attention. I'm pretty sure you had it already."

"I didn't."

"Mm-hmm, sure. We might have to start a Firebugs Anonymous for you and Abby."

Doc slipped quietly into the booth across from Thomas and dug into his pancakes while Riley went to make more toast. As sure as the sun rose that morning, the dial was turned to five. She wondered if she'd somehow moved it while cleaning the counter.

Moments later, an order came up for Meg. The only person not served in the restaurant was Luke, so Riley picked up the plated waffle and side of bacon and brought it over. She caught the tail end of an unpleasant conversation.

"I'm not interested in a relationship, Meg. You should set your sights on someone else. What about that guy you played pool with last night?"

Riley set the plate down and turned to walk away, but not before she heard Meg say, "He had a short stick."

For the rest of the morning and into the afternoon, Riley was subjected to suspicious stares from the patrons and abject disdain from Meg, who took up a seat in Luke's booth long after he left.

Like the queen she pretended to be, Meg ruled from her red pleather throne until Maisey walked in the door. Then she flew from her seat like her ass had caught fire.

"Busy morning, Maisey. Your niece tried to burn down

the place." Involved in her own tale, she didn't notice or comment that Maisey's bouffant was gone and in its place was a sleek, stylish bob.

"Oh my gosh, you look amazing." Riley walked around her aunt, taking the new cut and style in from all angles.

She cupped the curled ends. "You like?"

"It's so pretty." Riley reached up to touch her aunt's feather-soft hair. "Do you like it?"

It was obvious she felt pretty. It showed in the glow in her cheeks and the sparkle in her eyes. "I love it, but what am I going to do with that case of Aqua Net?"

"Don't get it near Riley. I hear that stuff is flammable."

Maisey turned to her. "What's this about a fire?"

Meg, with the dramatic flair of a seasoned thespian, described how Riley nearly burned the diner down by turning the toaster knob to five.

"That's funny, because when I left, I saw it was at two." She walked over to the toaster. "Let's fix this once and for all." She turned the knob to two and duct taped it into place.

"Meg was burned on her hand, Aunt Maisey." While Riley knew it was merely a ploy to get attention from Luke, she wanted to see how far Meg would go with the ruse. "She might need a few days off to recover."

"Oh, my goodness. Let me see." Maisey reached for Meg's hands, but she pulled them behind her back.

"I'm fine."

"Don't let her fool you. She said while it didn't look like much, it hurt really bad."

"Let me see," Maisey demanded.

After a frustrated exhale, Meg offered her hands to Maisey. "It's nothing. Probably the initial shock."

Maisey looked at Riley and smiled. "She's right, sometimes what doesn't look like much can be something more serious. I'll take the rest of your shift, and you can have tomorrow off as well."

"But..." She looked between Maisey and Riley, but the hate in her eyes was reserved for Riley.

"No buts. Off with you, now."

Meg stomped toward the back room and didn't return, which meant she'd taken the back exit.

"Why didn't you tell me she was treating you like cheap labor? I had to hear it from Dalton first, then Ben." She poured both of them a cup of coffee. "Come sit with me for a minute."

Riley looked around the diner. There were only two tables occupied, and they were happily eating their lunch.

She joined her aunt for a cup of coffee and a frank conversation. "I'm new. I'm learning my way around the town and the people. I don't want to rock the boat."

Maisey shook her head. "Sweetheart, you don't need to rock the boat, but you do need to drive it. Meg will strap you to a float and drag you behind if you let her. Don't let her." She reached over and laid her hand on top of Riley's. "There are drivers and passengers. You've been a passenger your entire life. Happy to sit in the back seat and let someone else determine your destination. When you got in the car and came to Aspen Cove, you became the driver. Where will you take yourself?"

CHAPTER FOURTEEN

Meg was like a sticky booger Luke couldn't shake off. He sat there at the diner and told her in no uncertain terms he wasn't interested in a relationship. At least not with her.

As he went over last week's calls and filed the paperwork, he thought about the toaster fire in the diner. Had it been two days since he'd been there? Two days since he'd seen Riley?

He had hoped she'd seek him out. That would tell him for sure she was interested in him. There had been no mention of their kiss, but he'd never forget it.

He'd kissed a lot of women in his years, but never had a kiss made his heart beat like a bass drum. The minute their lips touched, the heat between them was inferno-like.

"Fizzle, my ass."

"What's that?" Thomas walked in the office and took the chair in front of the desk. "Did you say you sizzle?"

"Nah, man." He replayed the entire conversation with Meg in his head. "Meg told me she's more fizzle than sizzle."

Thomas's eyes got big. "Meg claimed to be more fizzle?"

Luke set down his pen and looked up at his friend. "No, pay attention. She says Riley is more fizzle than sizzle."

"You disagree?"

Luke licked his lips, hoping somehow, he could remember the taste of hers. "Without a question."

"You've experienced Riley's heat?" He moved forward, folding his hands on the packet of papers he set down. "Like, her heat-heat?" He glanced down.

"Get your head out of the gutter. I'm not going to kiss and tell."

Thomas's head nodded slowly. "It all starts with a kiss."

"Says the confirmed bachelor buying a family home on a street called Pansy."

He sat back and frowned. "It gets me more bang for the buck."

"With your crazy standards, you'll never see any bang in that house."

"What standards? My only prerequisite is they have to be breathing and willing."

"Not true. Abby wants you."

"No, no, no. She raises bees. I'm allergic to bees."

"And commitment."

"True, I'm allergic to that, too, but it's not like there's a lot of options here."

Luke filed the last paper away and leaned back in his

chair. "What about that schoolteacher who lives on Daisy Lane? Mercy... Mercy Meyer, I think."

"No, no, no. She's a first-grade teacher. She likes kids. I'm allergic to kids."

Luke laughed. "There's Reese Arden. She house sits for her uncle Frank, the hockey coach. You like hockey, right?"

"I do like hockey, but she's a writer, which means she likes words, and honestly, I'd be afraid she'd talk my ear off."

"You're allergic to words, too?"

Thomas nodded. "Would seem so." He shifted his attention to the papers in front of him. "What do you think of this house?"

Luke rolled Thomas his pen. "Stop being a pansy, and sign the damn papers. It's not like you're going anywhere, and if truth be told, it would be nice to get you out of the firehouse on occasion."

"Why? You want to chase Riley around? Let her slide down your pole?"

"I know why you're single. It's not because you're allergic to anything. It's because you're an asshole."

"I'm that, too." He wrote his name at the bottom of the initial offer. "What about you? Are you going to rent that piece of crap on Bark Lane forever, or are you going to put down roots?"

"I'm in negotiations right now for a sweet piece of property. I'll let you know how it all goes."

"You do that." He rose from the chair and walked to the door. "I'm going to Doc's."

"That's a man of many talents. He can heal ya, kill ya, marry you and sell you a house."

"Currently, I'm only in the market for option four. The others..."

"I know, you're allergic to them."

Thomas pointed at Luke. "You're a smart one."

He nodded. "That's why I make the big bucks."

"Yep, and why you get to do all the paperwork."

Luke wanted to ask him if he was allergic to that, too, but he didn't want to beat a dead horse. Thomas was a good man. He was hard-working, thorough, and he never complained about anything except the lack of available women and the smell of James's dirty socks, which honestly could make a man faint.

Left to himself, Luke's thoughts went back to Riley. Maybe it was time to pay her a visit. His lips ached for another kiss. His eyes craved another look. His heart begged to have the blood pump like a raging river through it again.

He picked up his keys and walked over to the diner, hoping she'd be finishing her shift. When he got there, the only person he saw was Meg.

"Couldn't get enough of me, huh?"

"Meg, we talked about this. You need to set your sights on someone else. I'm not your man."

She groaned. "How do you know? It's like saying you don't like chocolate without ever trying it." She let her finger crawl up the buttons of his shirt until she tapped his chin. "Don't you want a taste?"

"Jeez, Meg, let it go."

She gave his chest a push, sending him back a step or two. "I bet you're not even that good a kisser."

Was she trying to use humiliation to get him to act? "Yep, you pegged me right away. I'm an awful kisser." *Did he dare take it up another notch?* "You thought the pool player had a small stick?" He walked toward the kitchen. "Is Dalton around?"

"You missed him. He's at the culinary school, teaching Basil Dawson how to debone a chicken."

"Now, there's a man for you."

"You think I'd be interested in a cowboy?"

He wanted to tell her he thought she'd be interested in anything with a job and a penis, but he didn't.

"He's handsome. He's motivated. He's a man who spends his days on the range. I bet he'd be an attentive boyfriend."

"Hmm, I like attention."

God help me. Luke pulled his wallet from his back pocket and took out two singles. "Can I have a coffee to go?"

"Sure." She picked up the coffee pot and poured him a to-go cup. "You know what they say?"

Luke poured a stream of sugar and a splash of cream into his cup. "I haven't got a clue."

Meg smiled. She reached up and tugged her ponytail. "Save a horse. Ride a cowboy."

He pressed the lid onto the Styrofoam cup and turned around.

"That's the way to rebound."

"I'm not giving up on you, Luke. I'm giving you a break from me. I'll be back."

Of course, you will. Thanks for the warning.

"See you later, Meg."

"I'm sure of it."

Luke walked out of the diner with one destination in mind—the Guild Creative Center. With any luck, he'd find Riley. Stopping to see Dalton was simply a shortcut to finding her.

CHAPTER FIFTEEN

Several large sheets of metal had been delivered to the studio this morning. Riley looked at the materials and let out a happy giggle.

Once she was organized, she'd get started on moving the design to the metal, then cutting them out.

In order to work efficiently, she had to know she was safe. Keeping the tanks at a reasonable distance from the work area was important. She'd asked her father to invest in longer connections so an accident like the one she'd survived at sixteen would never happen again.

She rolled the tanks close to the wall and unwound the cords and connectors.

In the center of the room, she put a long metal table and a couple wooden horses to support her work-in-progress.

On a table next to the wall, she laid out her smaller items —a box of wire and beads, pin backs and earring clasps, pliers, a small hammer, a soldering gun, and a small propane torch. The equipment she used to make jewelry and ornaments.

All the while, she thought about Meg. *Had she turned the toaster back to five?* It would have been nice to have a friend, but she wasn't sure where she stood with Meg.

"It's about Luke." She looked around the room and laughed at herself. Anyone looking from the outside would think she'd lost her marbles but talking to herself helped her analyze her life. The spoken words helped define situations.

"Does she hate me?" She lined up her tools like attentive soldiers. "Or does she hate that I've caught the eye of Mr. Sexy Fireman?" All she knew was Meg wasn't someone she wanted as an enemy if she could make her a friend.

Dalton had brought over a roll of butcher paper. She pulled out a six-foot length and taped it to the table in the center of the room.

Freehand, she drew the outline of a guitar and closed her eyes to imagine how it would look on stage.

"Fire." She sketched a few flames shooting from the neck. "Hot, smoldering...Luke."

How she'd melded Luke into her thoughts about the sculpture, she didn't know. Maybe because his kisses made her feel on fire, maybe because he had smoldering eyes and a mouth that could ignite her flame.

"Damn man, looks like a calendar model and kisses like a playboy." *Is he a playboy?*

"What if he kisses all the girls in town?" Riley touched her lips with her hands. "What if he kissed Meg and that's why she's mad at me?"

"I don't, and I haven't." His deep voice floated through the room.

She whirled around to find Luke leaning on the door, holding a pizza box.

"How long have you been there?" The heat rising to her cheeks was like an ember ready to flame. She feared she'd need a fireman to temper the burn.

"Long enough to know I look like a model and kiss like a playboy."

She opened and closed her mouth. What could she say? "It's rude to eavesdrop."

"Ruder to gossip." He pushed off the wall and walked into her space. When he got close, he set the box on the table and looked at her.

"I wasn't telling stories."

He rubbed the scruff on his chin, and the scratchy sound moved through the nearly empty space. "Fire. Hot, smoldering Luke." He said the words like an actor trying to seduce her with his low, gravelly voice. One brow lifted, as did the corner of his mouth, which shifted into a half-smile. "Will you deny it?"

"Oh my God, you were here for the whole thing. I was talking to myself."

"And what advice would you give yourself? You obviously like my kisses. Would you pursue another or sacrifice the pleasure for a friendship with Meg?"

"I was merely comparing your kiss to a far superior kiss. While you have rudimentary skills, you've got room for improvement."

"Is that right?" He took a step closer, placing himself inches from her body.

She hadn't realized how tall he was. Normally, he was sitting in a booth when she saw him. When he kissed her, she'd had several drinks, so everything was fuzzy.

"I had a few glasses of wine, which could have distorted my perception."

"For better or worse?"

"Hard to tell." All of a sudden, her mouth dried up like a desert. Her tongue was like coarse sandpaper scuffing the roof of her mouth.

"I'd like another chance to at least tie with the superior kisser. Who was he?"

Thoughts of kissing Luke again sent a flood of desire rushing through her.

"My brother's pug, Samson."

"Oh, hell no." He inched forward until they were chest to chest. Luke lowered his mouth to hers in a gentle brush of his lips before he crushed them against hers.

She had no choice but to submit. Not that she wanted to do anything else. The moment his lips touched hers, she opened her own in a soft moan.

A sweep of his tongue and the minty taste of him made her mouth water for more. A lash of his tongue against hers. A nibble on her lip. His hands wrapping around her body as if somehow, he knew her knees were but rubber bands.

Without a thought, her arms wrapped around his waist and her fingers traced the firm muscles of his back.

A rattling of keys broke them apart. They fell against the work table, out of breath.

"Oh, sorry." The lawman took in the whole scene. "Saw the lights on and wondered who was here so late."

"Hey, Mark." Luke wrapped his arm around Riley and led her toward the man in the sheriff's uniform. "This is Riley Black. Dalton's cousin." He turned to her. "This is Deputy Sheriff Mark Bancroft."

Riley had a brief moment where she wanted the cement floor to open up and swallow her, but she pulled back her shoulders and smiled. It wasn't as if she'd been caught doing something illegal.

"Nice to meet you, Sheriff."

He looked at her like she was in a line-up. Then his eyes went to Luke.

"So glad you found your own girl. Now you can stop pretending to be my wife's love interest."

"Oh." Riley slapped her palm to her chest. "I'm not his girl."

"No? You kiss everyone like a dieter sneaking a piece of cake?"

She wanted to react in shock, but his metaphor was too funny to ignore, so she laughed.

"Oh, the kiss." She nodded and glanced up at Luke. "I'm trying to help him perfect his skill set so he doesn't disappoint others."

"You keep telling yourself that." He took in the box of pizza on the table. "Hope you like your pizza cold." Mark left the studio; his laughter was heard until he walked outside the center and the door slammed behind him.

Riley's nose lifted and inhaled. The faint smell of baked cheese and bread scented the air.

"You brought pizza?" She knew it would be full of meat. If he offered her a slice, she'd have to turn him down because it wouldn't be nice to pull off the crust and toss the rest in the garbage.

"I did. I've kissed you twice and haven't once bought you a meal."

"Had I known that was the going rate for a kiss in Aspen Cove, I'd never go hungry."

"Don't sell your kisses so cheaply. They're worth far more than a meal."

"Depends on who you're talking to."

"I'm talking to you. How you see yourself is how others will see you, too." He looked around the room. There wasn't a chair in sight. "Can I use one of those?" He pointed to a stack of moving blankets sitting unused in the corner.

She chewed on his words of wisdom. Her experience was, how others saw her was how she saw herself. She glanced at the quilted blankets in the corner. "Knock yourself out."

He picked up one and spread it out on the floor. "Care to join me for a picnic?"

Everything in her screamed yes, but she wasn't sure. Sitting down for a meal would only give him a quick look at how different they were. She'd seen his plate at the diner—half-filled with bacon. "I'll join you while you eat, but I don't eat..."

He held up a finger and rushed to get the pizza box. With the flourish of a game show host, he opened it to show a vegetarian pizza.

"How did you know?"

"I asked." He walked to the blanket and took a seat, patting the space beside him.

It was a simple answer, but one she wasn't accustomed to. The concept of someone asking about what she liked was as foreign to her as speaking German or French.

"Wow." She sank into the spot next to him. "Not used to that."

He gave her an odd look. "Get used to it. You first." He held the box while she pulled a slice out.

"Do you like veggie pizza?"

He shrugged. "I'm not sure. I like bread, cheese, and vegetables. I'll pretend this is a combo without the meat."

Flexibility and consideration were also foreign to her.

"Are you a holder or a folder?" She looked at the slice he picked up and watched.

"Is there a right way?"

She bent the crust so the slice collapsed in the center, turning her piece into a makeshift calzone.

"No, but I like mine neat and tidy. Folding limits the risk of ruining my clothes."

He kept his flat and bit off the end. "I guess I'm a holder."

She thought of how he'd held her during the kiss. "Yes, you are. You're an amazing holder." She knew she must have had some dorky, dreamy look in her eyes by the way he smiled at her.

"We're no longer talking about pizza, are we?"

She took a bite and shook her head.

"Can we revisit your assessment of my kiss? I'd hate to fall second to a pug." He took another bite and chewed while he waited.

"No contest. You win. Samson uses too much tongue and saliva. When he kisses my face, I need a shower."

"Glad you don't feel the need for soap and water after me."

She tried on her bolder persona. "No, when I kiss you, I just want more."

He dropped his half-eaten pizza back in the box.

"Hold that thought." He rushed from her studio and returned with two bottles of water. After a drink and a thorough swish, he moved closer. Moments later, they'd forgotten all about the pizza. In a tangled mass of limbs, they fed each other kisses.

She had to admit he might be the best kisser she'd ever experienced. When her stomach growled, he pulled away.

"Appetizer is over. Time for the main course."

A surge of excitement arced through her. He seemed to like her kisses as much as she liked his. Could this be the start of something good? A flash of Meg's unhappy face flashed in her mind. Not wanting to ruin the moment, she tucked all thoughts of Meg away for later. "What are you offering?"

He rose from his prone position and pulled the box onto his lap. "Pizza, of course."

"Right." She picked up her discarded slice and took a

ravenous bite. Who knew kissing a sexy fireman could build such an appetite?

They sat on the blanket and ate pizza while Luke asked about her art.

"Sam wants two metal sculptures for the concert. Did she tell you about them?"

He shook his head.

The urge to begin drawing and cutting had her bouncing up and down like a kid waiting for ice cream truck money. Her arms became animated as she described how he would have to ignite the fireworks at the finale.

"I better not have to be shirtless and carry a puppy."

"Why would she do that?"

"It's my costume for the calendar. They have me wearing the bottom half of my turnout gear and holding a puppy."

"Aww, I love puppies."

He rolled his eyes. "What about shirtless firemen?"

She shrugged. "Don't know. I've never seen one."

He closed the pizza box and pushed to his feet. "Maybe next date?"

Her eyes shot open wide. "This was a date?"

"We had dinner, talked and kissed. Best date I've had in a long time."

He offered her his hand and pulled her to a standing position.

"What about Mark's wife? Did you date her?"

"Nope, she sat next to me at Cannon and Sage's wedding."

"Did you eat and talk?"

He turned his head and gave her a knowing look. "We did, but I never did this to her." He sucked the air straight from her lungs with his next kiss. It lasted long enough to make her dizzy.

When they broke apart, she stepped back and drew in a huge breath. "A warning next time might be nice. I can't breathe."

"I know CPR." He licked his lips and lifted his eyes in a flirty way.

"I may need it if you keep kissing me like that."

He gently pinched her chin between his fingers and looked into her eyes. "When I kiss you, I'll leave you breathless and wanting more."

He picked up the pizza box and walked out. He did as he promised. He left her wanting more. So damn much more.

CHAPTER SIXTEEN

The next few days kept Luke busy. A small forest fire broke out halfway between Aspen Cove and Cross Creek that kept the tiny firehouse hopping. He was always happy to help neighboring units.

Since he could remember, Luke believed good begot good. He supposed it was the same as believing in karma.

His team returned to the station, tired and covered in soot. Though the fire was out, their work would continue. The equipment needed to be cleaned and the rig washed.

"You going over to see your girl later?" Thomas pulled his helmet from the truck.

"My girl? She's about as much mine as you are Abby's."

Thomas groaned. "Not true. You've played tonsil hockey with Riley. I haven't gotten an arm's length next to Abby."

"That's by choice, although I don't see why not. She's pretty and nice."

Thomas shook his head. "She's also a woman of child-bearing years who no doubt wants marriage and kids."

"All right, Mr. Confirmed Bachelor, I'm rushing to the shower to get this crap off me." He wiped at the black on his face. "I'll be out in a few." He removed his turnout gear and dragged his tired ass to the showers.

It was amazing how soap and water could renew a man. He pulled on clean clothes and headed back to the rig to help his crew get it ready for the next event, which he hoped was a long way away.

James was winding the hose when he walked in. There was at least one man at the station at all times. Today it was James.

"Everything quiet?"

He nodded. "Mrs. Brown called, asking for you. She said she couldn't find Tom."

Luke chuckled. "Poor Tom most likely ran away."

"I went by and found him hunkered in the corner of the dormer window, dressed as a bat."

Luke couldn't imagine what that looked like. "A bat? As in flying, rabies-infected mammal, or wooden implement to hit a ball?"

"Black with wings. She's getting ready for Halloween."

"But that's months away."

James tucked the nozzle inside and stood back. "I'll never understand."

As Luke went to grab his gear so he could air it out and wipe it down, one of the alarms rang. When the station was built, it was equipped with automatic alarms connected to the

Guild Creative Center and a few other businesses, like Maisey's Diner. Eventually, they'd have the entire town wired so when a smoke detector went off, they got an alert.

James hit the alarm, and the crew rushed forward, jumping into their gear.

Thomas drove the rig while James hopped in the truck, and they sped with sirens blaring over to the Guild Creative Center.

Luke held his breath until they rounded the corner and saw no smoke billowing from the building. Didn't mean there wasn't a fire, but at this point, there wasn't a large event.

They rushed into the building, checking each unit until they got the end unit—Riley's unit.

He found her standing at the door with a folded piece of butcher paper in her hand, fanning the smoke from her studio into the hallway and toward the back door.

"You got a problem, ma'am?" he called over the loud alarm warbling through the building. He could see from his position a few feet away there was no fire, but there was certainly an exhaust issue.

He expected her to come back with some kind of funny retort. She seemed to have a lot of snark in her arsenal, but when he got closer and she moved the paper from in front of her face, all he saw were reddened eyes and streams of tears.

She looked at the crowd gathering around outside, peeking through her windows. His crew lined up behind him.

He turned to James. "Cut the alarm and tell everyone it's okay to return to their studios." James took off toward the back door, where the control panel was. Seconds later, the wail of the alarm stopped.

"I'm so sorry. I... I don't know what's going on. I was working, and all of a sudden there was a beeping noise, then a screeching sound. I'm so sorry. I'm so sorry."

He didn't understand the tears or the apologies. Nothing had happened. Did she think a fire alarm would send him running the other way?

He looked at his crew, who stood waiting for direction. "Give me the keys, James." James tossed him the keys to the truck.

Luke nodded toward Thomas. "Can you handle cleaning and prepping the rig?"

"I got it." Thomas took a few steps forward and glanced inside Riley's studio. "You want me to disburse the crowd?"

"Yes, please." Luke marched over to the windows and yanked down the blinds. "Show's over!" he yelled.

He wasn't sure the looky-loos could hear him through the triple-paned glass, but he hoped so, because if the building had been on fire, they would have been in the way. What was it about people and their need to rubberneck disasters?

Riley swiped at the tears in her eyes. "I've wasted your time."

He watched his crew disappear around the corner and pulled her into his arms. "This is my job. It's not a waste of time. Tell me what happened."

"I didn't start a fire. I was welding." She pointed toward the center of the room, where a piece of sheet metal was transforming into a guitar.

129

He had to admit, it was going to be amazing when she finished.

"Okay, was there a lot of smoke?" He took in the space around them. He had to give her credit. Her work area was tidy. The tanks were located far away from the flames. There weren't any obvious safety issues.

"No, not really. Metal burns fairly clean." She took in a deep, jagged breath. "Everyone thinks I'm a loser. It's a small town, and in five minutes there will be a rumor I burned down the Guild Creative Center."

He couldn't argue with her on that point. Small towns were notorious for gossip, but he had to give the people of Aspen Cove credit. They were a forgiving bunch and didn't generally rush to judgment.

"It will blow over."

She took a step back. "You don't understand. My whole life, I've been blamed for things I didn't do. I try and try, and bad luck follows me like a damn dark cloud."

Still dressed in his gear, Luke stripped down to the clothes he wore underneath, then returned to pull her into his arms.

"You can't be blamed for a fire when there wasn't one."

Rounding the door were Doc and Bobby Williams. They were still on the reserve roster and often came out to local calls.

"Heard there was a fire." One look at Riley wrapped in Luke's arms, and Doc continued. "Thought it had something to do with flames, not hormones." He turned to look at Bobby, standing next to him. "False alarm."

"Everything good here?" Bobby asked.

"Got it under control." He held her tightly.

Both men turned and disappeared, and seconds later Riley's knees gave way and she melted into the floor. A heap of tears and wails.

He rushed over to close the door to her studio, then came back, swooped her up from the cold cement floor and walked her to where the moving blanket still sat on the floor.

He lowered himself but kept her in his arms. She curled up in his lap like a wounded bird seeking refuge.

"Shhh, it's okay."

"No, it's not." She looked up at him. "You started this. You told everyone I was a safety hazard, and now they'll believe it."

He palmed her shoulders and held her far enough away for him to see her face. "I didn't tell everyone."

Again, she sucked in a jagged breath. "I heard you at the bonfire. You're a man of influence in this town. People will believe you."

"I'll set them straight."

She buried her face in his shirt. "You smell like smoke."

"Still?" He lowered his nose and inhaled. He didn't smell anything but her. Being next to her was like standing in the center of an orange orchard. "I showered."

She rose up and brushed her nose against his neck. "Okay, you smell like soap and cedar."

"Better than smoke." He scooted until his back was against the wall, then he cradled her in his lap. "Let's talk about what happened here."

She brushed the hairs that had escaped her ponytail from her face. "I told you, I don't know what set it off."

"That's not what I'm talking about, but let's address that first." He turned her so her back was to his front, but she still sat on his lap. "Did you turn on the exhaust system before you started?"

"The what?"

He chuckled. "There's our problem." He pointed to the wall and the knob next to the light switch. "This is a state-of-the-art building, and that is your exhaust system. It's designed to remove gases, smoke, and smells from the air. When it's not on, they build up and the system senses it. It probably beeped at you for several minutes before the alarm sounded, right?"

She nodded. "Yes, but I had no idea. I thought it was an air conditioner and the temp was fine, so I didn't mess with it."

"Problem solved. Next time, mess with it. Now, on to the next issue. Why so emotional?" He wrapped his arms around her middle, pinning her to him.

"I don't know."

"You do. What happened to my bold, beautiful woman?"

He could feel her swallow hard. "She's not real. She's someone I'm trying on for size. She seemed to fit until now. You seemed to like her, and now I'm not sure what you think."

He was glad she was facing away from him, or she'd see the shock in his expression. "I like you, Riley." He nuzzled her neck until her whole body shuddered against him. "Why are you so worried about what others think?"

She spent the next fifteen minutes telling him about her life. How her mother had left her and her twin brother when they were a month old. How her father needed a woman to help care for his children. How he'd married Kathy within weeks of meeting her. She talked about how her father left them emotionally long before he left them physically. He'd drowned his sorrows in a bottle of vodka before he drowned himself by passing out while doing dishes.

Her brother left when he graduated from college.

"Everyone leaves me. I have no one."

"Not true." He shifted her around so she straddled his legs. He wiped her wet cheeks with the pads of his thumbs. "You've got Dalton and Maisey, and you've got me."

He watched a twitch of a smile play at her lips. "You'll run as fast and far as you can once you leave here. Everyone does."

He pulled her forward until his lips were barely touching hers. "I don't run away. I run to. I'm not going anywhere, Riley." His hands skimmed her sides while his lips brushed hers. It was a tentative kiss. Not because he was unsure, but because he wanted to make sure she was on board.

When she rocked forward, her core against his growing hardness, he knew she was all in. He opened his mouth and tasted her sweetness.

Their tongues danced while his hands caressed all the places he could feel. When his fingers trailed across her back, she stiffened.

He pulled away. "You okay?"

She nodded. "Yes, I'm good."

"You want me to stop touching you?"

Her head shook. "No, I'd like you to touch me. God, I'm so pathetic." She let her head fall forward. "I'm starved for attention."

He cleared his throat. "Riley, I want you to be with me because you want me, not because you're starved for attention."

She gripped his shoulders like there was a chance he'd also abandon her.

There was no way he'd leave her now. He'd kissed her, tasted her, and somehow, she'd gotten into his system. She was as necessary as the blood that ran through his veins.

"I'm sorry, I'll be better."

He thumbed her chin so she was forced to look at him. "Be you. You're perfect the way you are."

"How would you know?"

"Because, sweetheart, I see *you*." He stared into her blue eyes and realized they weren't the color of a clear sky or tropical sea. They were speckled with green— a color he'd always associated with hope.

CHAPTER SEVENTEEN

It'd been two days since the incident at the studio. Two glorious days, or she should say two amazing nights.

The first night, Luke took her back to his place, where he cooked her an omelet and they curled up on the couch and watched scary movies. So scary she ended up in his lap, but she figured that was the plan.

Last night when she finished work, he was waiting outside, leaning against his SUV, dressed in worn jeans and a T-shirt.

He didn't tell her where they were going; he simply helped her inside the car and drove. Twenty minutes later, they were at a ranch. Ten minutes after, they were on a horse, her sitting in front of him. He took her to a vista, where they watched the sunset. Where he kissed all doubt from her mind she wasn't perfect the way she was.

Standing in front of the mirror, she slicked on her gloss and tucked the stray hair she couldn't get to behave behind her ear. She'd dressed in jeans because Luke always commented on how nice she looked when she wore them and paired the outfit with a button-down plaid blouse.

Luke was a country boy at heart. His story wasn't much different than hers, except he was missing the wicked stepmother.

"That's as good as it's going to get," she told herself. She trotted down the stairs and opened the door to find Katie struggling with a box in one hand and her toddler on her hip.

"Oh, my goodness. I need another set of hands."

"Let me help." Riley took the box since she had no idea what to do with a child.

Katie opened the door to the bakery and led her inside. "Put that over there." She pointed to the stainless-steel table in the center of the room. "I bought some rubber mats called Silpats. Maybe they'll stop Ben from burning the cookies. I swear, ever since your aunt got her hair redone, that man's brain has turned to mush."

"She definitely entered the twenty-first century with a bang. I love it." Riley set the heavy box on the table.

"Me, too." She looked down at her daughter. "Have you met Sahara?"

Riley took a step back. Children scared her. Only because she considered herself a poor candidate for motherhood, given her role model.

"No, but she's so cute." The baby propped on Katie's hip was a beauty. Golden ringlets hung down to her shoulders, and eyes that looked like a summer sky smiled back from the sweetest face.

"Sahara, this is your cousin Riley. Can you say Riley?" Katie moved forward and set Sahara in a playpen full of toys. "She doesn't say much yet. A few words like down and up, and of course dada and mumum. I'm not sure if the last one is her calling me or telling me she wants to eat."

Riley laughed. "Before you know it, she'll be talking your ear off and you'll remember the glorious days when she had a vocabulary of four words."

"No doubt." She looked to the ceiling. "Everything good up there for you?"

"Yes, in fact. I'm making good tips at the diner, and I'd like to pay you something."

Katie was already shaking her head before Riley finished her sentence. "Not necessary. How could I charge you for something given to me?"

"Easy. Heck, I paid three hundred dollars a month to live in the space above my dad's workshop, and it didn't even have a kitchen. I microwaved everything."

Katie's hand went to her mouth. "Oh my gosh, another microwave wizard. You and Sage will have to get together and compare notes. I don't think she's ever cooked anything that couldn't be nuked in under ten minutes."

Speaking of time, Riley looked at the clock. "Oh, shoot. I'm late for work. I gotta go." She dashed out the back door.

She was at full run when she pushed through the diner door to find Meg leaning against the counter.

"You're late." She grabbed a pack of cigarettes from under the counter. She turned but dropped her lighter.

Riley rushed over and picked it up. It was white with a fifties pin-up girl on the front. "Sorry. I was helping Katie." She handed the lighter to Meg.

"Maybe you should help yourself first. You could use all the help you can get." She spun on her heel and walked through the swinging doors, no doubt heading outside for a smoke.

Aunt Maisey came through the doors looking a bit disheveled. Her hair was mussed, and her lipstick was smeared. She looked back over her shoulder. "Did you twist her knickers again?"

Riley took her freshly laundered apron from her bag and tied it around her waist. She popped her head inside the door and tossed her purse on the nearby table.

"She hates me. I don't know what I did." She looked around the mostly empty diner. "That's not true. Today, I know." She pointed to the clock. "I'm late."

"Late night with Luke?" Her aunt's voice sounded hopeful.

"No, that's not why." She shook her head, hoping to settle her brain cells in place. "I did have a date with Luke, but I was late because Katie needed help with a box."

"That's fine, sweetheart. Meg will get over it." Maisey grabbed the pot of coffee. "I'll make the rounds and meet you in the corner booth."

She couldn't let her aunt deliver coffee looking like she'd been kissed good and hard.

"Wait up." Riley took a napkin and cleaned off the orange color that bled past her lips. "How much is Uncle Ben wearing?"

Maisey leaned over to look at her reflection in the shiny new toaster. An addition since Riley had managed to start two toaster fires since her first day. She was certain she wasn't responsible, but she couldn't prove otherwise. After the alarm incident at the studio, she'd gained the nickname 'Cinder,' which was fitting, but not when it came to flames.

"That man." Her tone was serious, but her face had a smile that could light up the room. "I love that man." She pointed to the booth in the corner. "You take a seat. I'll bring the coffee."

Riley did as she was told and took a seat in the booth. She watched her aunt make small talk with Doc and Agatha before she moved on to the tourist who sat by the window.

When Maisey approached her, Riley turned over two mugs. "Am I in trouble?"

Her aunt reached for the sugar jar and tipped it over. It appeared she liked a little coffee with her sugar. She knew a sexy fireman who took his coffee exactly the same.

"No, you are not in trouble." She stirred the coffee.

Riley was certain the spoon could stand on its own with so much sweet sludge at the bottom.

"It's Meg, right?"

"Does something have to be wrong for me to want to sit with you?"

"Umm..." Her head nodded. "In my experience, 'have a seat' means you're getting canned or verbally caned."

Maisey laughed. "Nope, no cans or canes. Although I wanted to ask how you're doing." She lifted her brows. If she'd had her shellacked bouffant, her hair would have shifted with them, but her sleek bob stayed stylishly in place.

"I'm good. I like it here. It's a huge change for me." The biggest change was she truly felt like she was coming into herself. She could be the free spirit her cells screamed to be and not be chastised.

"Yes, I bet it is." She sipped her coffee and grimaced. After another helping of sugar, she said, "Meg doesn't think you're cut out to waitress."

"So, it is a caning." It took everything in Riley not to curl up like those hard-shelled pill bugs.

"No, I think you're doing a great job. I've not heard one complaint. My intention is to simply ask if you're happy."

How she felt wasn't something she'd considered before she came to Aspen Cove. She wasn't entitled to express her feelings, but here, she'd found out what happy truly meant. Happiness came in sweet goodnight kisses at her door. Tender hands that rubbed her back when Luke hugged her. It was a shoulder broad enough to support the world. An erector set that sat on her coffee table. A town that seemed to have accepted her despite the fact they thought she was a fire hazard.

"I am happy. While Meg isn't happy with me, I like what I'm doing. I like the town and its people. Besides, the tips keep me in macaroni and cheese and microwave popcorn."

"Just checking, because if you're not, we can find you

another job. Ben and Dalton could always use a hand cooking."

Riley considered having to cook things she refused to eat. "I'll pass on the cooking unless there's an animal-free zone."

"Nope, we bake 'em, poach 'em, grill 'em and fry 'em. I'm surprised you can serve what we cook."

"It's not that I'm against other people eating animals. I've eaten a few burgers in my days. I don't enjoy the experience."

Maisey craned her neck to make sure her customers were doing okay. "Does it have anything to do with Kathy telling you that you had an ass as big as a water buffalo?"

"You remember that? I was eight. She put me on a diet. I weighed sixty-seven pounds then."

"I don't like to talk poorly of the dead," Maisey said.

Riley squinted her eyes and tilted her head. "She's not dead."

"She is to me." She stood and patted Riley's head. "You're perfect the way you are. All ninety-seven pounds of you."

"One hundred and thirty-two pounds," she threw back.

"Go eat some fries." Maisey picked up the coffee pot. "You and Meg play nice, now. See you tomorrow." She walked through the swinging doors, leaving Riley alone with Meg.

A family of four walked through the door. "Evening, all," Meg said in her saccharine voice. She led them to her station, sat them at a booth and walked away. "Be a dear and take their order for me, will you? I need to run down to the corner store and get some cigarettes."

That's how the rest of the day went. Meg found a reason to disappear when work arrived and managed to show up to pocket the tips.

Riley could have been angry, but there was a positive side to a disappearing Meg—nothing caught fire today.

CHAPTER EIGHTEEN

"Can you hold the puppy lower so we can get a good look at your stomach muscles?" Poppy moved her light and stood over him before she took the shot.

Luke lay on his back, his pants pushed low on his hips, his yellow coat wide open to reveal his bare chest while a fluffy ball of white fur scampered up to lick his face. He laughed as the puppy tucked under his chin to take a rest.

"Oh my God, I couldn't stage that any better. Hold still." The shutter of her camera ticked in rapid succession. "Stay there. You're Mr. February, so we need more." She dashed away.

Luke brought his hands behind his head and closed his eyes. Thoughts of Riley rushed through his mind. They'd seen each other every night. Dinner, walks, kisses, lots of feels, but each night ended with him walking her home and kissing her on her doorstep.

Something told him she'd never been cherished or valued. It seemed as if she'd been used and taken for granted her whole life. He refused to be another person who would hurt her.

"Don't open your eyes. This shot is perfect."

He stayed still while something dropped onto his stomach. Softness and prickliness touched his skin at the same time. "Is that a rose?"

"Good nose," she said.

"No, I feel the thorns." It was a good thing, because he could focus on the sharp edge of the thorns rather than his hard-on. He had his gear on, which would hide his burgeoning desire. He'd had at least a half-dozen ice cold showers since he met Riley.

"I hear you're dating Maisey's niece." The shutter clicked again. "How's that going?"

He opened his eyes.

"Don't move."

"If you don't want me to move, then stop asking me questions." The puppy shifted and rolled from under his chin to the ground. Then snuggled up to his side.

Poppy had been taking pictures all over the firehouse. His shoot was in the garage in front of a locker, where all their turnout gear was stored. His team would have loved to stand in the background and wisecrack, but Poppy had kicked everyone out.

"I'm a girl. I need information."

Luke shifted on his side and pulled the puppy close to his chest. "It's going well. I like her. I think she likes me.

144

We'll see." He leaned down to kiss the top of the dog's head.

"Hold that." Again, the clicks sounded in rapid succession. "That's the one. It's perfect."

"Where did this guy come from?"

"Charlie borrowed some pups from the humane society in Copper Creek. We're giving them a cut of the profits. Why? Do you want him?"

"I'd take them all, but I can't have a puppy right now. I'm still trying to figure out how to manage a girlfriend."

Poppy let her camera drop to her chest. "Riley's your girlfriend? That's a lot more than dating. Girlfriend implies exclusivity and commitment."

Luke sat up, transferring the pup to his lap. His big hands gently petted the animal. One of his palms almost covered the tiny thing.

"We haven't talked about it, but I'm not seeing anyone else. She's not seeing anyone else. She's a girl and my friend. Girlfriend fits perfectly."

Poppy smiled. "I like her. You chose well. So much better than Meg."

"I've never dated Meg."

"Not because she didn't want to date you. That girl's been on you like lint on tape since you came to town."

"Not interested, but I think she could teach your brother Basil a thing or two."

Poppy gasped. "Don't even think about it. She'd chew my brother up and spit him out."

Luke lifted his brows. "Not a bad way for a man to go."

He snuggled the puppy once more, then handed him back to her. "Take care of this guy." He lifted the puppy up and looked more closely. "I mean girl."

"Will do. We have Thomas tomorrow, then we're fini—"

An alarm sounded, and Luke pushed to his feet. Thomas came in with a smile on his face. He tossed Luke his T-shirt.

"It's zone eight at the GCC. Your girl is up to no good." He started toward the gear locker.

"I got this. If I need you, I'll call." Without changing, Luke tucked the T-shirt Thomas had thrown him into his back pocket and walked outside.

He climbed into his personal vehicle and headed towards trouble packaged as a blonde. When he arrived, he saw her kneeling down before the metal frame she was welding, the bright light almost blinding to the naked eyes.

She'd attached the guitar to wheels so it could move easily.

Focused on her work, she didn't see him reach inside the door and turn on the exhaust fan. The beeping that would no doubt turn into a screeching wail went silent. With his shoulder against the door frame and her body shielding the bright light of the arc, he watched her in awe. She was fearless when it came to heat and metal. He thought about how far she'd come since she'd arrived. Too bad she couldn't manipulate Meg like she did steel.

He cleared his throat loudly as he walked forward. She turned her head and stopped. Seconds later, she killed the flame and stood, taking off her protective mask.

"Oh my God, I did it again."

"Yes, you did." He moved forward so they were inches apart, both in fire protective gear, only his was open to reveal a bared chest.

She gave him a hungry look, then glanced behind him. "Is everyone else here, too?"

He shook his head. "Nope, just me."

She set the gun down and removed her gloves. Her hands roamed up his stomach to touch his chest. It wasn't the first time she'd had her hands on his bare skin, but somehow this was far more intimate than the rest. Maybe it was the look in her eyes. The way she chewed the inside of her cheek. Her hair all sweaty and mussed, like they'd already been in bed for hours.

He shifted to give his rise room to adjust.

"You always answer calls half-naked?" Her thumbs brushed over his nipples, causing him to hiss. He was sure there was a direct line between them and his aching length.

"Only when the call is to my forgetful girlfriend."

Her smile was so big and bright he swore it rivaled the brilliance of her welding flame.

"Your girlfriend?"

"You have a problem with that?"

"No, I like it." She ran her lips softly across his chest, kissing him until she reached his neck. "You like this?"

He threaded his hands through her hair and kissed her. He didn't need to tell her how much he liked it; he'd show her.

His body pressed against hers, backing her up until she was flat against the wall, with nowhere to escape.

She tugged at his jacket until it dipped off his shoulders. When he dropped his arms, it fell to the floor, leaving him nude from the waist up.

"Your turn," he said. He yanked the zipper of her overalls down and tugged until the brown material hung around her waist. He'd caressed her skin and cupped her breasts, but he hadn't seen her naked.

"You want to do this here?" She looked around the studio. The blinds were still pulled, but the door was open.

"Sweetheart, I want to do this everywhere with you. We can start here."

"Close the door and lock it."

He didn't need any more coaxing. He had the room locked down in seconds.

They met at the quilted moving blanket, where Riley shrugged out of the overalls, leaving her in jeans and a T-shirt.

Luke sent a quick text to Thomas, telling him all was fine, but he'd be gone the rest of the night.

When he looked at Riley, he saw fear in her eyes.

"You okay?" He dropped to his knees and pulled her close to him. "We don't have to do this today, or here."

She shook her head. "It's not that. I want you. I want this." She lowered her head. "More than anything. It's just that...I'm damaged."

He didn't know what she was referring to. "What do you mean?"

She scraped her bottom lip with her teeth. "Promise me you won't turn and run."

He cupped her face. "Nothing will make me run from you, Riley. Nothing." That might not have been the truth. If she dropped her pants and was sporting the same equipment as him, it would give him pause.

While he had lots of friends whose taste went in many directions, he preferred the lush curves of a woman. The soft, wet glove of her body hugging his length.

She gripped the edge of her T-shirt.

He'd been in many precarious situations in his life. He'd faced walls of flame and imminent death, and never had his heart beat so wildly.

"Tell me what you're afraid of, sweetheart."

"I'll show you." She lifted her shirt to reveal soft, milky white skin. It rose to show a white, lacy bra cradling perfect breasts. She cleared her head and tossed the shirt aside.

"You're perfect." He reached forward to cup her breasts, but she shook her head, stopping him midway.

"I'm not. The other day, you said you saw me. I need you to see me." She reached behind her and unhooked her bra. The material fell free, and in front of him the most beautiful set of breasts swayed back and forth.

"Riley, if this is damaged, I want you to be a wreck always. You're so damn beautiful, I can hardly breathe."

She held up a finger. "Wait." She turned around and showed her back.

He held in the gasp rising from his throat. Sitting on his heels, he rose to his knees to close the distance and reached out to touch the scars that marred her perfect skin.

Her muscles flexed under his touch. "How?"

"My first lesson in safety. You think I'm not focused on safety. I might forget to turn the exhaust on, but I'll never let what happened to me happen to anyone else."

She told him about the accident and how her stepmother told her no one would want her because she was ruined.

Luke sat down and pulled her into his lap. One hand cradled her scarred back while the other cupped her cheek. He thumbed the tear that slipped from her eyes.

"This doesn't matter to me. In fact, it makes you all the more beautiful because you're strong." He moved his fingers over the grid-like scar. It was almost a perfect three-by-three. "I can't imagine what that felt like. I work with fire, but I've never truly been burned."

"Not fun at all. Sometimes it still hurts. In the winter, my skin gets dry and tight and the pain ghosts back into my life. What hurts worse is the pain of her words. She hated me."

He laid her down and looked at her beauty. It wasn't only on the outside. Her loveliness ran marrow deep.

"You know, I'm falling deep and fast for you." He tugged at his uniform pants until they were stuck at his ankles. After kicking off his boots, he was able to slide out of them.

Her eyes fell to the swell of his erection pressing against the denim of his jeans. "Looks like you haven't changed your mind."

"I told you I wasn't the type to run away, but the type to run to. I'm here, Riley, and I want you. All of you, from your beautiful smile to the laces of your tennis shoes." He moved over her, his chest as bare as hers. Both were clothed from the waist down. "We can wait. Make it special. You know, candles and flowers and some fancy vegetarian fare."

She tugged at the button of his pants. "Or...we can make it real. This is who we are. I'm an artist. You're a fireman. Let's see what we can create together."

CHAPTER NINETEEN

Under the bright lights of the studio, they tugged at each other's pants until they laid themselves bare for each other.

He seemed fascinated with her breasts while she was captivated by everything that was Luke.

He spent his time working his mouth from her ankles to her neck and everything in-between. The man was a great kisser, but that tongue had talents of its own.

He tasted her body and groaned, telling her she was the perfect mix of salty and sweet.

Her hands roamed every inch of him. He was a man of contrasts, from his soft skin to his hard length.

They didn't rush into the act; they built up a frenzy of passion that had her body shaking each time he touched her.

With his tongue and fingers, he brought her to the edge so many times her muscles ached from the fatigue.

"Please," she begged. She lifted to see him kiss her inner thigh. His tongue was like a heated lashing against her skin. When he drew his mouth to her needy core, she held her breath, knowing the minute she quivered on the edge, he'd pull away, but he didn't.

He licked and suckled until her knees shook and her insides burst into flames. It was like riding a roller coaster through the heat of hell, only to soar into heaven.

Ripples of pleasure moved through her body like a stream heading into rapids. The roiling rough waters washed away any thought that she was damaged.

When her thundering heart settled down to a steady beat, he climbed between her thighs. He reached for his pants and pulled out a condom. She watched him expertly roll it on in a microsecond.

Pressed at her entrance, he looked down at her with such love in his eyes. Heavy-lidded and full of passion, the green had grown deep and dark, like nature-made emeralds.

"You're perfect, Riley, perfect for me." In a single, steady thrust, he filled her up. She lowered her hands to his hips and held on while he moved inside her.

"God, it's so damn good," she said and meant it. Luke was an all-in kind of man. He made love with his whole body and made sure she felt loved on every inch of hers.

Slow, lazy strokes made her want to melt into the blanket. Hard, forceful thrusts sent her soaring. She matched his movement. Copied his rhythm. They were like a finely tuned instrument.

She tried to flip him over but was no match for his strength.

"My turn to work your body. Your turn to lie back and feel."

He smiled and flipped them over so she straddled him. Though the floor under the blanket was hard on her knees, the feeling of having him deep inside her compensated for any discomfort she experienced.

He gripped her hips and set the pace he liked. Up and down she moved until she saw his jaw flex and his eyes close.

Two could play at his game. She rose onto her knees, pulling him almost completely from her body. When she heard him growl his displeasure, she sank fully onto his rod.

"Jeez, Riley. You're trying to kill me."

"No, I'm making sure you feel good. Making sure you'll remember this moment for a long time. I want you to want it so badly that, like me, you'll beg." She leaned forward and nipped at his lips.

"I'll beg you right now. Please put me out of my misery."

She laughed. "Not yet. I haven't had my fill of you."

"Careful, sweetheart. Those words give me lots of ideas."

She teased and tortured him until he was begging her. When she wouldn't relent, he used his strength to take control.

She found herself on the bottom again. His powerful thrusts urged her body to peak again.

"Are you getting your fill?" He leaned down and pulled a taut nipple into his mouth.

The tingling started at her toes and moved its way to her

sex. A shift of his position gave her the extra friction she needed.

"Holy shit," he called out as her muscles tightened down on him. The tiny flutters turned into vise-like spasms that coaxed him over the edge. Together, they found their pleasure.

In a tangle of limbs, their sweat-covered bodies came down from the high. He tied off the used condom, setting it aside, and spooned next to her. His fingers mindlessly caressed her skin until goosebumps rose.

"Are you cold?"

She rolled into him, putting her face against his chest. "No, I'm perfect."

His fingers traced the scars on her back. "Yes, you are."

They both dozed off for a few minutes, but it was Riley who shifted away. She stood and looked down at the sleeping man in front of her. His body was a work of art. She had run her tongue over his stomach at least a dozen times. Reveled in the way it dipped in and out of troughs of muscles. She knew he was built, but nothing could prepare her for how her heart flipped at the sight of him now.

He told her he was falling hard and fast, but she'd already fallen, and she never wanted to get up.

Luke stirred. His eyes opened halfway. "Are you leaving me?"

She dropped to her knees and bent over to kiss him. "Never."

He let out a sigh of contentment. "I thought you were going to sneak out and leave me here naked on your floor."

Luke didn't have an ounce of self-consciousness; then again, he was made by the gods himself.

"I was watching you sleep. Better than a movie. Thought I'd step out for popcorn and come back."

He rolled to his knees and grabbed for the T-shirt that was still shoved in the pocket of his work pants. "I'm starving. How about we get a bite at the diner and take a walk?"

"You're feeding me again. I guess this was a date?"

He rose to his feet and hopped into his pants. He folded up his gear and stepped into his boots.

"Every minute I'm with you feels like a date." He looked down at the blanket and smiled. "Best damn date I've ever had."

"Me, too." She turned toward her sculpture. "Let me get everything put away." She gave him a wink. "You know, safety first and all that."

"How about I go find some real shoes and meet you at your place in fifteen minutes?"

"That will work."

He wrapped his arms around her and gave her a spine-tingling kiss. "It's fifteen minutes too long, but I'll see you soon."

She almost blurted out, "Love you." Didn't know why it was on the tip of her tongue, because she'd never said those words to anyone except her brother and father.

She tidied up her workspace, making sure the hoses were rolled up and put away. She double checked the power and unplugged the equipment. Better safe than sorry.

She barely made it inside her place before she heard the

light knock on her door. It dawned on her Luke had never been in her apartment.

She trotted down the stairs and let him in. "Come up for a second. You can check out the apartment while I change my clothes."

He followed her up. "Damn, this is nicer than my rental."

She smiled. "Your rental is great." She walked into her bedroom, shedding her clothes along the way.

"Is this an erector set?" he called from the living room.

"Yep, my first welding project, although I used a soldering gun. Got the whooping of a lifetime because it wasn't only mine. Baxter was half-owner."

She rummaged through her closet. She didn't have many clothes. With a pink dress and yellow one in her hand, she debated between them.

"The pink tonight, the yellow tomorrow." He leaned his head on her shoulder and kissed her neck.

"You're like a cat moving soundlessly through my place."

"I like your place."

"You can stay the night if you'd like." She hung the yellow dress back in the closet and put on the pink.

"I'd like that."

Once she'd washed her face and slicked on some gloss, she was ready.

Hand in hand, they walked across the street to the diner. Meg was pulling the night shift.

Riley went to pull her hand away from Luke's, but he held on tight. "You're my girlfriend. I'm happy to let everyone know."

She laughed. "Everyone doesn't have access to an array of sharp knives."

"I think she's more bark than bite."

He led Riley to his favorite booth, the one he always sat at when he ate there.

"When they find me dead, you'll know where to look first." She slid into the booth and expected him to slide in the bench across from her, but he scooted her in and took the space beside her.

The swinging doors flew open, and Meg walked in. She stopped in her saddle shoes and let her mouth fall open. Once she tucked her shock away, she pasted on a smile and walked over.

"Hope you haven't been waiting long." She held up her pinup girl lighter. "Bad habits."

"Just walked in."

"Together, I see." She leaned her hip against the table and pulled out her order pad. "What will it be, handsome?" Meg looked at Luke as if he were alone.

"I'll have a diet soda." He turned toward Riley. "What about you?"

"Water is good for me."

"Boring." Meg leaned in to Luke, but her voice wasn't a whisper. "When you're ready to up your game, you know where to find me."

Luke turned away from Meg and looked at Riley. "You look beautiful."

Meg pushed off the table. "If you're into Earth Mother, with a touch of Barbie."

Once Meg knew they wouldn't be nibbling at her bait, she left to get their drinks.

"Someone is getting poisoned tonight, and it's not you."

He pressed his soft lips against hers. "Nor you. She's like a kid throwing a temper tantrum. Don't be afraid to fight back."

She shrunk. "I'm not much of a fighter."

He wrapped his arm around her. "No, you're one hell of a lover."

When Meg returned, she took their order. A grilled cheese sandwich and fries for her, and a double cheeseburger with onion rings for him.

They enjoyed quiet conversation while they ate.

When Meg dropped off their check, she leaned against the back of the bench across from them.

"You don't eat any meat?" she asked Riley.

"Nope, I don't eat meat of any kind."

A hateful smirk crossed Meg's face. She turned her attention toward Luke. "You poor thing...that must mean blow jobs are completely off the table."

Riley tensed until Luke set his hand on her thigh. "While she might not eat meat, she seems to enjoy my cucumber."

Both women were stunned into silence, but it was Riley who responded. She shoved her hip into his until he moved from the booth.

"Both of you are awful." She looked at Meg. "You because you're selfish and spiteful, and you..." She whirled around to face Luke, "because even though you see me, you've not heard a word I've said."

She was too angry to be hurt. She marched out the door and across the street toward her apartment.

She mumbled to herself while she walked "First you make me the town firebug, and now you make me the town whore."

CHAPTER TWENTY

"Dammit." Luke wanted to chase after her but needed to pay the check. He tossed two twenties on the table and took off out the door.

She was rounding the building when he caught up with her.

"Riley, hold up." He chased her all the way to her door. "Can we talk?"

Her hands were shaking so badly she struggled to get her key in the door. When they fell to the ground, she sank to the cement with them.

"Why would you do that?" She turned her back to the door and brought her knees up to her chin, tucking the fabric of her dress around her bottom.

"I thought I was defending you."

She looked up at him with saucer-sized eyes. "By telling her I enjoyed your cucumber?"

Hearing it come out of another mouth made it sound worse than how it played out in his head.

"I was claiming you. Telling her you belonged to me."

She pushed out her legs, forcing him to shift to her side. He leaned against the door and slid down to take a seat beside her.

"All you told her was you gave me something she's wanted all along. She and I are two dogs after a bone."

He chuckled. "I'm the bone."

Riley tried to stop the laugh bubbling up inside her. "Apparently not. You're a cucumber."

He shouldered her gently. "You like cucumbers."

She leaned into him, pressing her head to his shoulder.

"I like yours, but the entire town doesn't need to know."

Luke was glad he hadn't angered her beyond repair. If she was willing to joke with him, then what they had begun together wasn't lost.

"I'm sorry. I hated the way she badgered you, and on some level, it was a slight against me, too. As if, somehow, your dietary preferences would count me out. My intention was simply to toss back what she was dishing out."

She wrapped her hands around his bicep. He loved the way her touch warmed him all over. They were in the middle of a disagreement, and still, her touch was loving and tender. There wasn't a mean bone in Riley's body.

Her chin lifted, and she looked up at him with eyes that spoke a thousand words in a single glance. Words that said she didn't trust but wanted to. She didn't want to fight with him but had to stand her ground. She didn't want this to define them.

"If you're going to be my boyfriend, you have to understand the dynamic of my life."

"Tell me what I need to know."

She looked over her shoulder at the door. "You want to come upstairs?"

He hopped to his feet and offered her his hand. "More than anything." He pulled her to her feet. Without letting go of her hand, for fear she'd change her mind, he bent over, picked up her keys, and unlocked the door.

They had two doors to get through before they were in her apartment. The bottom door led to the bakery and upstairs to her apartment, and the upper door let them inside her place.

"I have coffee, water, and juice."

He didn't want anything. All he wanted was to iron out this wrinkle between them. He sat on the blue couch and patted the spot beside him.

"I want you to tell me how to be a better boyfriend."

She sank into the spot beside him. She played with the applique flower on her dress. "All my life, I've been an outsider. Even in my own home. All I want is to belong somewhere."

He slid his arm over her shoulder and pulled her close. "You belong to me." In his heart, he knew that to be the honest truth. Riley Black came to Aspen Cove looking for something, and she found him.

"When my dad died, the first thing Kathy did was put the

house up for sale, which meant I no longer had a place to live."

"You're twenty-seven. Why were you living with your parents?"

She smiled. "I wasn't freeloading. When the shop burned down, my father had it rebuilt with a studio apartment on the second floor. He wanted me and Baxter to have a place to land if we needed one."

"You needed one?" It was obvious at this point he and Riley didn't know much about each other. They'd exchanged the compulsory information about age, food likes, dislikes, favorite colors, but she was right, he didn't know much about her family dynamics except her stepmother sounded like an awful person.

"No, but my dad wanted me close by. I think I always acted as a buffer for him. He felt better if I was around, so he offered me the place."

"What did Kathy think about that?"

"She thought it was great because she could charge me rent."

"How did you earn money in Butte?"

She got a sly smile on her face. "I was a professional produce tester. You know how I like those cucumbers."

"Oh, so now it's a joke." How funny that a few minutes and some clarity could turn something hateful and hurtful into something funny. Life was all about perspective.

"Seriously though, I did work at a grocery store stocking produce, so it's not too far off the mark. On weekends, I helped my father."

He hated she sat next to him, where he couldn't easily read her expression, so he maneuvered her so she straddled his legs and looked into his face.

"This is what I've got so far. You had a mean stepmother. Your brother left you when he went off to college and never came back. Your father abandoned you to a bottle of booze until he died."

She shook her head. "That about sums it up, but Kathy wasn't mean, she hated me."

Luke set his hands on her hips. "How is that even possible when you're so loveable?"

"You tease, but she literally hated me. She was kind to my brother and tolerant of my father, but me..."

"Did you ever ask her why she was mean?"

She shook her head. "No, why would I?"

"To get answers. I found everyone looks at things through a different lens. We all see the same scene but have different versions. I wonder if she truly hated you or if you misinterpreted her intentions."

Riley pulled back, and he was positive she would leap off his lap, so he tightened his grip on her hips.

"Are you taking her side?"

He moved his hands around her body and clasped them together, locking her in place.

"No, but my dad always told me there were three sides to every story. There was your side, my side, and the truth, and no one is lying."

"What the hell does that mean?"

"Everyone has their own truth and motivations. It might

serve you well to ask her what her problem with you was. Maybe it's not what you think."

She looked past him like she was contemplating his words. "I never thought about her motivations. I assumed it was because somehow, I took something away from her. Maybe I looked like my mom, or maybe my father gave me too much attention."

"You'll never know until you ask. There's no risk. She's out of your life, so if she gets angry, she's still out of your life."

"You're right. It's that her words are so hurtful. It was always 'You'd be pretty if only...,' 'You'd be more successful if only...'"

"Listen to me. You're perfect the way you are. While you see yourself as damaged and flawed, I see you as a beautiful woman with so much to offer."

"It's a good thing you're sight-impaired." She poked at his shoulder in jest.

He hated to bring up Meg, because she was the one who started it all. "You have to learn to ignore Meg. Find your armadillo shell and let her barbs and verbal bullets bounce off you."

"Easier said than done."

"Sweetheart." He leaned forward and rested his forehead on her breastbone. "She's a professional asshole, and that skill isn't on your resume. Don't try to go toe-to-toe with her. Her words lash out from her hurt."

"I suppose you're right. Don't all of our actions come from our experiences?"

"Yes, and you want to know what actions I want to act on?"

She pressed her core closer to his growing erection. "You want to show me your produce?"

He rose from the couch with her, wrapping her legs around his waist.

"Nope. I'll make you a carnivore yet, even if it's only in bed." With her wrapped around his body, he walked her to her room.

Once there, he set her gently on the bed and stared down at her. He hoped his expression conveyed the emotions in his heart. He was falling hard for this woman. He loved her sweetness. Loved her ability to forgive. Loved she was willing to listen to reason. Loved her warrior spirit.

Riley might think of herself as weak, but how many women would pack up what they owned and drive to a strange place to begin again? In that way, they were so much alike.

"You know what I love about Aspen Cove?" He crossed his hands, grabbed the hem of his shirt, and pulled it over his head.

"The people?"

He shimmied her dress up her thighs, over her hips, and peeled it from the rest of her body. He tossed it aside in the same pile as his shirt.

"Yes, but it's more than that. This is a place where your dreams can come true. It's where a small-town man came to be a fire chief. Where a pop star came to fall in love. Where a girl who hadn't spoken a word found her voice. What do you want, Riley Black?"

She reached up and gripped the belt loops of his jeans. "You, Luke Mosier. I want you."

"You've got me. I'm yours."

Her smile was bright enough to light the room. "I don't think anyone has ever truly chosen me. You did."

He made quick work of undressing himself and rolling on a condom. With a quick tug from her hips, her lace panties joined the other clothes on the floor. He moved between her open thighs and entered her in one smooth stroke.

He relished the sound that rushed from her mouth. It was a cross between a sigh and an ohhh. Her body fit him like a second skin. Hugging him tight and pulling him deeper. Once fully seated, he stopped all movement and waited for her to look at him.

"I'll always choose you."

THEY MADE love several times that night. When her alarm rang at seven, they climbed out of bed and showered.

They moved around her kitchen like a well-oiled machine despite not having been there before. He made toast while she brewed coffee. He buttered the bread while she pulled out the jam. At the door, they gave each other a kiss like they'd done it a thousand times before.

He walked to the fire station while she headed across the street to work. These feelings he had for Riley were foreign to him. The way his heart ached when she walked away scared the hell out of him.

When in doubt, he always called his brother.

"Twice in a month?" Cade answered. "What the hell? You okay?"

Luke smiled. "Yep, better than okay. I needed some woman advice."

Cade's laugh echoed through the phone. "Don't forget, I date sheep. This isn't my lane. Call Trinity."

"Have you ever been in love?"

There was a moment of silence. "Dude, you need to call Trinity. I'm not the person to talk to when it comes to love."

"Okay, but I'll never hear the end of it. Are you sure you don't have any advice?"

"I got plenty of advice. Run in the other direction, and if she manages to catch you, make sure you get a prenup."

Cade had been single for a long time. He'd married his high school sweetheart. Things were good for the first year until she decided she wanted stilettos instead of cowboy boots. She left him for their attorney.

"Sorry to bring up old wounds."

"No worries. Besides, that crap's been scarred over for a decade or more. I'm a confirmed bachelor."

"We'll see."

"You want to know about love? Call our sister, she'll set you straight." There was a pause. "Oh, and before you go, you know of any ranches nearby looking for some help? I'm a bit tired of the racehorses. I want to get back to moving cattle."

Could Luke's life get any better? He had a beautiful girlfriend, and the possibility of his brother coming to Aspen was icing on the cake.

"I'll text you Lloyd Dawson's number. He owns Big D Ranch and could use a hand."

"Big D sounds like the perfect place for me. Size does matter."

"Whatever. I'm calling Trinity."

He hung up with Cade and dialed Trinity.

"Hey, big brother. What's up?"

He swallowed hard. It was a hit to his ego to call his sister, who was six years younger, and ask about love.

"You ever been in love?"

Her laugh started low and ended in a pitch that hurt his ears.

"At least a hundred times. Why?"

His sister never seemed to be alone, but he'd never considered her to be serious about anyone. She treated relationships like a change of clothes. When one got old or worn or out of fashion, she'd trade them in for another.

"Seriously, how do you know if you're in love or in like, with a high dose of lust thrown in?"

He could almost see her chewing her lip.

"Can you imagine your life without her?"

He hadn't thought much about it, but he did know his life was sweeter with her in it.

"That's not a good litmus test. You can live without anyone if you have to."

She groaned. "You asked."

"I need something solid."

"Okay... would you do anything for her? Give up something you love for her? Put her needs before yours?"

"Yes," he answered without question.

"You're in love. Who is she? What's her name? What does she do? I need a picture. Will she make a great sister?"

Trinity peppered him with too many questions.

"Riley, she's an artist, I don't have a pic to send, and I think she'd make an awesome sister."

There was a squeal from the other end. It was so loud, he had to hold the phone away at arm's length.

"When's the wedding?"

"Don't rush things."

Luke walked into the station and made his way to his office, where James sat with his feet on top of his desk. He pushed them off. "Don't you have something else to do?"

"Hey," his sister said, "you called me."

"Not you, Trin. James has decided his ass belongs in my chair and his feet belong on my desk."

"Oooh, James? Is he cute?"

Luke chuckled. "If you like stray puppies."

"I love puppies. Send me a picture."

"Goodbye, Trin. I love you."

"I love you, too. I'd love you more if I got some pictures."

He hung up and looked at James.

"Is there a reason you're in here?" Luke wasn't territorial about his space, but it was odd to see James sitting at his desk.

"Nope, I'm hiding from Thomas." He peeked around the corner. "I was trying to save time and tossed my clothes in with his. Who knew his whites would turn pink?"

"You turned all his tighty whities pink?"

"Like bubblegum."

"James!" Thomas roared from the garage. "You owe me."

James dove under the desk. "I'm not here unless your sister wants to talk to me. I can be her puppy. Does she look like you, or is she cute?"

"Thomas," Luke called. "He's in here, cowering under the desk."

CHAPTER TWENTY-ONE

It had been several days since Riley ran out of the diner with her hair on fire from internalized rage. Since then, she'd thought long and hard about what Luke had told her. She'd turned and churned the words in her head while she worked around the clock to complete the sculptures for the benefit concert.

Somewhere in-between was where the truth lay. That's what Riley took from their conversation. Kathy's truth, Riley's truth, and the real truth. Meg's version, her version, and the actual facts.

When she walked into the diner after nearly no sleep, she found Maisey prepping coffee filters while Meg stocked the condiment shelf. Things had been tense for them, but with her aunt's constant presence, there wasn't much time for snark on Meg's part, but plenty of opportunity for dirty looks and sabotage. Things like salt in the sugar and other high school-age pranks were a daily occurrence.

In order to have a good work experience, she and Meg needed to come to an understanding of sorts, even if it meant they never spoke to each other.

"Mind if I steal Meg for a moment, Aunt Maisey?" A nervous warble filtered through her voice. She wasn't confrontational. Her mode of operation was generally to cave to pressure, curl in on herself. She'd often retreat before conflict could arise. To confront the issue was a new experience but one she'd need to conquer in order to survive. Maybe that had been her problem all along. Maybe she'd left it up to others to defend her, and if they didn't, she settled into her role as martyr.

Her aunt gave a head tilt and then a nod. "Don't kill each other."

"Not planning on bloodshed," she teased.

Riley told Meg to grab her cigarettes and come out back with her. She knew the woman wouldn't miss a chance to take a break.

Standing behind the diner with the forest as their backdrop, Riley began.

"I know you don't like me."

An unlit cigarette dangled from Meg's lips before she set it alight. One big drag and a cloud of smoke later, she spoke.

"It's not that I don't like you. It's simply you have the things I want."

Riley leaned against the wall. This was a new experience for her. In Butte, no one would have been jealous of her.

"You mean Luke?"

She took another long drag, but this time Meg blew the smoke into the air rather than Riley's face.

"It's more than that. You have an awesome aunt. You've got the apartment across the street. You've got the studio, and yes, there's Luke. Must be nice to have everyone give you something." She flicked her ash to the asphalt.

"It is nice, but it's not something I'm used to. My whole life, I've fought for what I got. Moving to Aspen Cove was the change I needed." She almost hung her head in shame, as if the life she lived wasn't deserved. That needed to change, so she pulled back her shoulders and held her head high.

"What do you want from me? You already got it all. What could I possibly give you?" Meg tossed the cigarette butt onto the asphalt and ground her heel against it.

"I was hoping we could call a truce. That maybe if we set aside our jealousies, we might be friends."

Meg lifted her plucked thin brow. "You're jealous of me?"

In reality, there was nothing about Meg that Riley coveted, except maybe her black and white saddle shoes, but she knew she had to toss some flattery the woman's way, or things would never move forward.

"Sure, you're pretty, and you always look so darn cute in your pinup girl outfit. You make more money in tips, too." That was because she stole half of Riley's, but mentioning that would set them back.

Meg moved her head so her ponytail would swing back and forth. "I told you to show your personality and the tips would be good."

She looked down at her average-sized chest. "I fear you have a lot more personality than I do."

Meg laughed. She cupped her indecently exposed girls and shook them. "So much damn personality."

"Can we start over?" Riley took a step forward.

"You already have my man. So no, but we can move forward from here." Meg pulled Riley in for a hug and nearly crushed her. "You think you can get me a date with Thomas?"

They turned and headed in the door.

"No, but I can put in a word."

"A good word," Meg said as she tossed her lighter and cigarettes on the table.

Riley tagged her aunt, who pulled the early shift. She usually arrived around four to open the place at five for the commuters and the long-haul truckers who stopped in.

"Doc's order is in, and Luke arrived." Maisey untied her apron and kissed Riley on the cheek. "Have I told you lately how proud of you I am?"

"Yes, and thank you." There wasn't a day that went by where Maisey didn't have a kind word for her. "Love you."

"Love you more, sweetheart."

"Love you most," Riley replied, and her aunt rolled her eyes.

Dalton slid Doc's pancakes out the order window. "How's the art going?"

"It's going. I'm working day and night on it. It will be close, but I'll have it ready."

She could have made them less realistic, but what was the purpose in showcasing a piece that wasn't her best work? She wanted the instruments to play. Who wouldn't want to strum a six-foot steel guitar? Getting the frets and the strings right was her biggest challenge.

"Your boy toy is in. Why don't you wait on him this time? I'll take Doc his cakes." Meg picked up the plate and left.

"What did you do to our Meg?"

"I asked for a truce."

"Wow. Who knew that was all it would take?" He turned from the window to cook the next order.

Riley headed over to Luke with a pot of coffee.

He turned over his mug. "What time did you leave?"

He hated that she left him in bed in the middle of the night, but she couldn't help it. There was no way she'd fail the people who put such faith in her.

"Three." She pulled her hand to her mouth to cover her yawn.

"Look at you, you're sleepwalking."

She looked around the diner to make sure everyone had what they needed. "I'll be all right."

Luke reached out and took her hand. "I care about you, and I'm worried you'll get hurt. People cut corners when they're tired."

"I'm almost finished. A couple more days, tops."

Meg walked over, and Riley looked up to see how she'd react to Luke and the public display of affection. They'd been careful not to throw gas on the fire when it came to Meg.

"Hey there, Luke." She tossed an envelope on the table in front of him. "Doc says you're all set. Whatever that means."

Luke let out a whoop and fist pumped the air. He glanced past Meg to where Doc sat and gave him a thumbs up.

"What's going on?"

He looked directly into Riley's eyes, completely ignoring Meg. "I bought some land to build a house."

She knew he hated the rental he lived in. The place probably should have been condemned. The plaster crumbled when it was touched, and things dropped from the ceilings and walls all the time. Last night as she left, the doorknob came off in her hand.

"Land?"

Luke looked between the two but settled his eyes on Riley. "I wanted to surprise you. How would you like to wake up to a water view?"

"Oh my God. Really?"

He slid the papers over and grabbed both of her hands. "I bought the lot next to Dalton and Sam's place. Thought maybe you could help me design a house."

"There you go again. Getting it all." Meg's eyes narrowed as if the idea irked her, but then she smiled. "Congratulations, you two. That sounds fabulous." She picked up the coffee pot Riley brought over. "You should rest a bit. You've been burning the candle at both ends for far too long."

Riley looked at her. "How do you know?"

Meg shrugged and walked away.

"That one is still trouble," Luke said.

"True, but she's nicer trouble now."

They forgot all about Meg while Luke told her about the

property. "I'm meeting Noah Lockhart here to talk about the timeline and get his ideas on house plans that would fit a waterfront property."

"Noah Lockhart? Isn't he the guy I talked to at the bar? Tall. Dark. Handsome."

Luke frowned. "I don't know. I've always thought he looked like a troll mated with a sasquatch."

Riley reached over and slugged him in the arm. "Luke Mosier, are you jealous?"

He lifted and sat beside her. "How can I not be? I have the most beautiful girlfriend." He rubbed the dark circles under her eyes with his thumb. "Even the raccoon look favors you."

"Flattery will get you everywhere—later."

"I'm counting on it."

She shifted her hip to scoot him from the booth. "I've got to get to work, or I'll use up all my nice points with Meg in one morning. You want bacon and eggs, hash browns, and wheat toast?"

"I want you, but I guess breakfast will have to do."

She left the booth but snuck in a quick kiss. "Yes, for now."

"Any chance you can skip the studio tonight and have dinner with me?"

"Nope, but I promise after the concert, I'm all yours."

"Baby, you're already all mine. After the concert, I might see you more."

How wonderful that sounded. Although her schedule

was crazy right now, they managed to find time for each other. Luke pulled his all-nighters at the station, and she'd stop by when she finished at the studio. When he came off shift, she was often back at the studio, so he brought her coffee and a muffin from the bakery.

If they managed to fall into bed together, she generally snuck out early to get a few hours in at the studio before she pulled her shift at the diner. So far it was working, but she could see the want in his eyes. Her heart ached to be with him.

The bell above the door rang, and Noah Lockhart walked in. His eyes swept the room, looking for Luke. Once he found his target, he moved like a guided missile.

"Hey, Riley. Looking good."

"Yes," Luke said. "My girlfriend is sizzling hot."

Noah shook his head. "Good for you, man. You snagged a good one. Pretty. Smart. Although not too smart if she chose you."

"You want your coffee in the mug or in your lap?" Riley asked. "One more quip about my intelligence, and you won't get a choice."

Luke laughed. "That's my girl."

She slipped the order into the clip and spun the wheel. "Order up."

"Forget Thomas. I'll take him." Meg lifted her chin toward the front corner booth. "Noah, right?"

Riley leaned against the counter and looked to where Noah and Luke sat talking about building his dream home.

She couldn't believe he'd bought the land. She was more shocked he wanted her input.

"Noah Lockhart. Be careful though, he's got the reputation of a player."

Meg picked up the coffee pot. "I like to play." She sashayed her way to her next victim.

CHAPTER TWENTY-TWO

It had been three days since he and Riley had slept in the same bed. He'd been called out to several big fires in the area. Thankfully, none close enough to Aspen Cove to put the town in danger.

Living in a mountain town made the risk of fire ten times worse. Tall pine, fir, and spruce made crown fires hard to fight when they jumped from tree to tree. His small crew was doing all they could to help the Silver Spring department put out a fire started by a careless camper.

The one thing Luke couldn't tolerate was carelessness.

He shed his smoke and soot filled clothes in the laundry room of the fire station.

Thomas walked in wearing his pink underwear and a T-shirt.

"You know, you can buy new stuff. You make a decent wage."

He looked down at his bubble gum-colored skivvies. "I'd rather buy tile for my new house than underwear. Besides, this is a great reminder as to why clothes get sorted. Hey, James," he yelled. "Come here." He tossed his dirty clothes in the washer and pointed to Luke's soiled ones. "You want those washed?"

James walked in. He looked at Thomas, and his jaw tightened. The muscle in his temple started to tick. "What?"

"Luke and I have laundry, and I thought you'd like to get started on it."

James stomped forward and swept the clothes from Luke's hand. "Jeez, how long will I have to pay for turning your shit pink?"

Thomas shrugged. "I don't know... maybe until you learn you never wash red with white."

"I got it."

Thomas mussed up James's hair as he walked by. "Great, then this is your last load."

Luke followed him up the back staircase to the bunks, where they all stored spare clothes.

"Tile, huh?"

Thomas tugged on his jeans and slipped into a pair of black boots. "I'm going neutral. All beiges, whites, and browns with hints of yellow. Hardwood floors. Blinds instead of drapes. Getting the damn popcorn ceiling removed." He pulled a black cotton shirt over his head. "How's the planning coming along for your new digs?"

"It would be coming along faster if Riley was around to give her input."

"Still burning the midnight oil?"

"She's burning oil around the clock. With the concert in less than two weeks, at least there's an end in sight."

"You're crazy about her, aren't you?"

"Either I'm in love or I'm crazy." He bent over and tied his shoes.

"You're in love, and that makes you crazy."

"Such a cynic. You should try it sometime, it makes you feel all warm inside."

Thomas pulled on his jacket. "I'll stick to Irish coffees. Gives me the same feeling without all the hassle. Cheaper, too." Thomas waved goodbye and walked out of the room. "See you tomorrow."

Luke looked at his phone to see if Riley had responded. He'd sent her a text telling her he was on his way home. No response meant she was hard at work.

He left the firehouse and headed for home, thinking he'd grab a bite to eat, then go to the studio.

When he pulled into the driveway, his heart rate picked up. There was Riley, sitting on his front step, wearing her white flowy dress and looking like a damn angel.

He threw his SUV into park and raced to her. Seeing her sitting there waiting for him was the best reward for a long day.

"Hey beautiful, I didn't expect to see you here."

She rose to her sandaled feet and wrapped her arms around him. "I missed you. I feel like I've been neglecting you."

"I missed you, too, but I understand your need to finish. Won't being here put you behind?"

"Yep, but I'll make it up. Besides, you're worth it." She squeezed him tight.

He could get used to having her there with him all the time. Hell, she was with him regardless. Riley was the first thing on his mind in the morning and the last thing on his mind at night.

"Do I smell like a barbecue?"

"You sure do, but I like barbecue."

"Liar."

She shook her head. "No, you haven't had anything until you've barbecued a portobello mushroom or a cauliflower steak." She threaded her fingers through his hand and followed him into the house.

"You can't call that barbecue."

"I just did." She moved in the direction of the kitchen. "How about I make us some supper and you take a shower?"

"So, I do stink."

"No, I love the way you smell, but I can see the tension in your shoulders, and the ash in your hair has given it a gray tint. I have to say, when you turn gray, you'll still be hella hot."

"That sounds like an amazing plan—dinner, not turning gray." He gave her what he hoped was a toe-curling kiss. Something of a promise of what was to come later.

They parted ways in the kitchen.

For the hundredth time, the handle to the hot water fell off and clattered to the bottom of the chipped porcelain tub.

Luke was so glad he'd purchased the land. He'd be even happier when they broke ground on the building.

Noah was excited to share a greenhouse plan his buddy Owen Cooper had been perfecting. In all honesty, it was the perfect idea since the house would face east and get full sun most of the day. Solar-powered, it would leave a small footprint on the world and a smaller dent in his wallet.

He wanted Riley's input because he wanted her there with him. He wanted her always. If things continued to go as well as they had, it would be her house, too.

Wearing sweatpants that hung low on his hips and a T-shirt that stretched tight across his chest, he walked barefoot into the kitchen.

On the stovetop was a pot of bubbling beans. Next to it was the package of no-lard tortillas and a pouch of grated cheese.

He'd never considered eating vegetarian but often did when he and Riley ate together. He had to admit the food was always good.

"Smells great."

She whirled around, sending her dress floating around her sexy legs.

"Yes, you do."

She moved over and leaned against the faded Formica counters. "How do you look so yummy in sweatpants?"

"It's a gift," he teased.

She turned off the stove and moved toward him like a lion hunting prey. That look in her eye made him immediately rock hard.

"How hungry are you?" She splayed her fingers across his chest, making sure to skate across his sensitive nubs. "I only ask because if you're a gift, I'm eager to unwrap you."

Luke never said no to the chance to be with her. Be inside her. They moved slowly back to his room, leaving their clothes along the way. He made slow, passionate love to her because that's exactly what it was. He was head over heels in love with her.

As they lay in post-lovemaking bliss, he took a deep breath because the time had come to move things forward.

He rolled to face her, setting his hand on her rounded hip.

"I have a question."

"I'll give you an answer." She traced the curve of his jaw.

"I've been thinking about us."

No one had a prettier smile than Riley. It was the kind that lit up her eyes and brought color to her cheeks. He was certain when she was happy even her hair looked shinier.

"I love the way we play house together. Love how coming home to you makes me feel whole. I was hoping you'd move in with me. I know it's soon, but everything about us feels right."

When her smile fell, so did his heart.

"I want to. I do, but if I lived here, I'd never get anything done. With the concert rushing towards me, I can't afford to get behind." She traced her finger down his chest to his happy trail. "You're a huge distraction."

Even though he wasn't happy, he laughed at her huge

comment. "If I had a shorter, less impressive hose, you'd consider it?"

"Such a fireman." She rolled him to his back and straddled him. If she wasn't careful, they might not get to the food she'd prepared for a while. "Tell you what, I'll stay over as often as I can, and if you feel the same way after the concert, ask me again, and I'll say yes."

"Okay, so you're moving in after the concert. Shall we start bringing your things over now?"

She positioned him at her entrance and eased down onto his length.

His questions were replaced with moans. He couldn't think, much less talk when he was deep inside her. They'd given up condoms for a safer form of birth control. The problem was... skin on skin, and he had no control.

Later that evening, they sat on the couch eating cold bean and cheese burritos.

"Are you leaving me as soon as I fall asleep?"

"Nope, I'm curling up next to you and sleeping like a baby."

He kissed the top of her head. "You make me happy."

"You make me horny."

He picked up their empty plates. "Time for bed, then."

CHAPTER TWENTY-THREE

Riley managed to swing by her apartment and change before her shift at the diner. She tossed on a pair of jeans and threw on a pink tunic. She wrestled her hair into a ponytail on her way out.

Each time she passed by the erector set, she smiled. When she was a kid, she'd told everyone she would grow up to be a metal artist. No one but her father had faith she could accomplish that goal.

Her fingers skimmed the metal frame as she walked past. She had made it. She'd walked through fire and come out the other side a better person. When the concert took place, her art would take center stage. It was like a private showing.

She trotted down the stairs with happiness flowing through her veins. Life had taken a severe right turn for her. One day she was living above her father's shop, the next she was being kicked out, the next she had a place in Aspen Cove, and now she had a studio, a job, and a boyfriend. She hated to jinx her luck by thinking about it, but damn, she'd hit the jackpot.

She wouldn't be late, but she wouldn't be early either. Walking through the door of the diner, she figured she'd be on the dot. Meg, no doubt, would be tapping her toe and looking up at the clock to see the big hand snap to the twelve.

When she looked up, there was only her Aunt Maisey, who'd managed to turn her stylish bob into something big and stiff and unattractive.

"Mornin', darlin'." Maisey tossed her a clean apron. "Meg's out back, taking a cancer break."

"Bad habit, but we all have something we can't kick." For Riley, that something was Luke.

"She says you've turned into a decent waitress. Did you pay her to say nice things, or are you two best buddies now?"

"No payment necessary. We're grown-ups and talked out our differences."

"If you say so. In my experience, women are catty or batty. Some are both; those are the ones to watch out for. Crazy and jealous is never a good mix."

Riley wasn't sure what Meg's motives could be for being nice. All she knew was, being friends with Meg was far more pleasant than the alternative.

The bell rang above the door, and Luke and his crew walked inside. From the back emerged Meg. She always seemed to have her radar set for Luke, or maybe now it was Thomas since she'd changed targets.

"Sit where you'd like, boys," Aunt Maisey sang out.

Luke looked at Meg, then at her. She could see the reasoning going on in his brain. He wanted to sit in her station, but to do so might upset Meg since he'd always sat in her area. He rocked left and right and then walked toward his regular booth, with James, Thomas and Jacob following.

"Why don't you take care of them? I mean, he is your man."

That confirmation made Riley heat up inside. "Are you sure?" She looked toward the table. "Thomas is there, so I thought you might want to wait on them."

Meg leaned over and took a peek. "He's good looking. No doubt built. Probably good in bed, but he's made it plain and clear all he's looking for is a good time."

Meg's answer puzzled her. "Wasn't it you who said you liked a good time?"

"No. We were talking about Noah Lockhart being a player, and I said I liked to play, but I also like to win, and there's no winning with a man like Thomas."

Another man walked into the diner. He was tall and every bit the cowboy. "You take him," Riley said.

"Oh, Lord have mercy. I bet that man can give a good ride." Meg swept the coffeepot from the burner and walked away.

Riley bounced over to the firemen's table. Since it was no secret she and Luke were an item, she bent over and kissed him.

James made some sordid comment about sliding down the greased pole, but Thomas grabbed his ear and told him he was back on laundry duty. Maybe he'd learn how to sort out and clean up his dirty mouth.

After four orders of pancakes and bacon, they finished up and left, but not before Luke gave her another kiss.

The cowboy was still there, and so was Meg. She was practically sitting in his lap. Her blouse had popped an additional button to show off her ample personality.

After noon, Aunt Maisey and Uncle Ben left, leaving Dalton, Meg, and Riley to handle the afternoon. A few of the locals were picking up shifts here and there as well. Even Louise Williams took two shifts a night. She said it was her quiet time, but in truth, it was probably because eight kids drank a lot of milk and they needed the extra cash.

By the end of the day, Riley was dragging, but she had so much to accomplish.

Meg was helping her with her side-work and chattering on about her cowboy, Wyatt, a new addition to the Dawsons' ranch.

"You know what they say: spare a horse, ride a cowboy."

"You got a date?"

Meg laughed. "Not with him." She wiped the counter and tossed the towel into the nearby bucket of soapy water. "You and I have an after-work date at the Brewhouse." She reached behind her and untied her apron. "Don't say no, or I might change my mind about liking you." She rolled up her apron and shoved it into her hiding spot next to the full ketchup bottles. "As soon as Louise shows up, come on over."

Meg was gone before she could argue. Riley didn't have time for a drink at the bar. She didn't have time for much of anything. She had to weld the guitar strings in place, as well as the firework holders. She had some chemical treatments she wanted to apply to give the metal the deep patina she was after.

On the other hand, she knew if she didn't show, she'd be back to working the place by herself and dealing with burned toast and anything else Meg could conjure up to make her life miserable.

She shot a note to Luke because she didn't want him to think she was choosing Meg over him.

I've been shanghaied into having a drink with Meg after work.

She leaned against the counter and waited for his reply. It came right away.

Is she blackmailing you or just being nice?

The bell above the door jangled, and in walked Louise.

Both but I'm only staying for a soda and then I'm off to the studio.

"Hey, Louise," Riley said. "I'm thinking Doc might be in since he didn't show for lunch, but it shouldn't be too crazy." Riley took off her apron and folded it nicely. She always put hers on the table in the back. If it was there, it always got cleaned.

"Not sure of that," Louise said. "I hear Charlie went into labor. It's a bit early for them. They were hoping to get a few more weeks in, but I suppose thirty-seven weeks is good when you are carrying two."

"Oh, my goodness. We're going to have more babies in town."

"Thank goodness, because Bobby and I can't populate Aspen Cove on our own." She gave Riley a sly smile. "We did try though."

Louise took over, and Riley rushed to Bishop's Brewhouse to find Samantha on her way out.

"Hey, I was going to call and ask how the sculptures are going?"

Riley had asked her not to peek because she wanted them to be a surprise. "They're great. I'm putting on the final details. In fact, I'll be heading over after I have a drink with Meg."

"You think that's wise?"

"What? A drink, or a drink with Meg?"

Samantha glanced at the table, where Meg sat waiting. "Both?"

"I'm sticking with soda, and Meg... well... that's a work in progress."

"I'll see you later, then."

When Riley sat at the table with Meg, she was already halfway done with her first glass of wine.

"What'll it be?" Cannon called from the bar.

"A Coke, please."

"Really?" Meg said. "You come to a bar for a soda pop?"

She pulled out the chair and sat. Immediately, the orange cat raced over and did figure-eights around her legs.

Meg looked down and frowned. "Why does everybody and everything like you better than me? That cat hisses at me when I try to touch it."

Riley wanted to tell her animals were a good judge of

character, but that would have been the kind of snark Meg dished out, and she didn't want to be Meg.

"He's only got one eye, so maybe you caught him unaware once, and now he's cautious." Neither of them believed that, but they let it slide on by.

"Tell me about your work at the studio. I keep hearing about these metal sculptures."

Cannon brought over her drink. After a sip, Riley told her all about her work as an apprentice to her father, who did more industrial welding but supported her artistic side. She was happy to share that with Meg, who looked bored but never once interrupted.

"After my father died and my stepmother sold the property, I came here."

"Lucky us," Meg said. She dug into her purse and pulled out her cigarettes and lighter. "I need a smoke." She popped out of her chair and walked toward the back door.

Luke walked inside. He found her immediately in the almost empty bar and came to sit beside her.

"I wanted to see you before you left for the studio." He leaned in and gave her a kiss.

Cannon walked up with a beer and a cup of coffee. "Are you on? Drinking or no?"

Luke reached for the beer. "I'm off duty. Thomas and James are at the station."

"Laundry duty?" Riley asked.

Luke chuckled. "No doubt." He glanced around the bar. "Slow tonight. I'd have figured Sage and Doc and Bowie would be here."

"The twins are on their way. Sage, Lydia, and Doc went with Charlie to the hospital in Copper Creek. Bowie went as moral support to Trig."

Riley took a drink of her soda. "I'm a twin."

Cannon's eyes grew wide.

"Identical?"

"Nope, my twin has a penis. His name is Baxter."

"I can't even imagine having twins. That's got to be so hard on the mother. What about yours? How did she survive having you and your brother?"

"She didn't." She looked up at Cannon. "She abandoned us. My father was looking for a mother for his kids. Kathy was looking for a man with a job. We were pawns in a marital negotiation."

Luke pulled her in and kissed her head. "I would have paid anything for you."

Cannon laughed. "You got it bad, buddy. No cure either."

Luke lifted his mug of beer. "Thanks, man. What about you? Any babies in your future?"

Cannon let out a playful growl. "It took me years to get her to the altar, but I'm hopeful. I hear babies are contagious."

"You two are talking like babies and love are leprosies."

"No way. All I'm saying is, when you find the one you love, you want it to be eternal. Who wants to fall out of love?"

"Not me," Luke said and blushed.

"Did you tell me in a roundabout way you love me?"

He pulled the mug of beer to his lips. "Pleading the Fifth."

"Hmm, you're playing hard to get."

He leaned over and whispered in her ear, "I'm hard, but when it comes to you, I'm easy."

"For everyone, or only me?"

"You're it for me."

A shadow was cast across the table, and they both looked up to Meg's frown, which immediately turned into a smile.

CHAPTER TWENTY-FOUR

"Ah, loverboy is here." Meg took the empty seat next to Riley.

Luke was happy to see she was respecting boundaries. A week ago, she would have climbed into his lap.

He gave her a cursory nod. "Meg."

"You're squeezing into girls' night out."

Beneath the table, he set his hand on Riley's thigh and watched her face for a reaction. She always had some kind of response to his touch. A smile. A sigh. A moan. Tonight, it was a smile.

She turned to look at him. "Missed me already?" Leaning into him, she laid her head on his shoulder.

All the while he looked at Meg, whose easy demeanor hadn't changed except for the tic in her clenched jaw. She reached into her purse and pulled out a twenty, placing it on the table. "I've got to run, but I'll see you both soon." She shouldered the strap of her purse and left.

"Wow, what happened to the Meg we all know and loathe?"

"She's all right. Maybe she's misunderstood, like most people."

Cannon walked over and picked up the dirty glass and the cash. "It's surprising to see her leave alone. I was ready for her to pull out the gloves and fight Riley for you."

Luke sipped his beer. He scooted his chair closer to Riley. "Meg must have finally figured out she would have never had a chance." He turned to look at her. "How could she when I'm in love with Riley?"

The mention of love silenced them all. It was Cannon who spoke first. "I'm all about the love." He turned and walked away, leaving them to ponder Luke's confession. While they had joked about it earlier, he hadn't actually said the words, but now that they were out, they felt true and right.

"You do love me." Riley's smile was like high beam headlights.

Luke shrugged. "I think you're all right."

She shouldered him and laughed.

He waited for her to say the words back. Her love was evident in the way she looked at him, the way she kissed him, the way her body talked to his when they made love.

As she opened her mouth, Cannon walked back with a bottle of wine. "Let's toast to love." No sooner had he poured them a glass, all hell broke loose in the bar with the arrival of Trig, Bowie, and Doc.

Trig stood in the center of the room and threw his hands

in the air. "I'm a dad to two beautiful, healthy boys." He pounded on his chest like a caveman.

Besides Luke and Riley, there was only one other patron in the bar. Luke didn't know the man well, but he recognized him as Tilden Cool. The man had been present both times old man Tucker's stills blew.

What always struck Luke as odd was Tilden appeared to be educated and refined. He couldn't understand why he'd be hanging around the town's bootlegger.

"Congratulations," Riley said. She rose from her chair and hugged the new father. "What did you name your boys?"

All three men pulled up chairs around Luke and Riley's table.

Cannon came back with frosted mugs and a pitcher of beer.

Trig took his phone from his pocket and showed off his beautiful boys.

"This handsome guy is Jonah. He's the firstborn. He came out screaming like a banshee." He scrolled to the next photo. "This is Jason and he didn't make a peep. Everyone was worried, but he was fine. It was as if he was taking it all in. They suctioned out his mouth, and he took a big breath, scrunched up his face like he would scream to the heavens, but then he closed his mouth and appeared to look around."

Luke picked up his glass of wine. "Here's to the love of a fine woman and the blessings she brings to her man." He tapped his glass with the men and turned to face Riley. "I'm so happy you're mine."

Trig continued to show pictures of his children. He even

showed one of Charlie holding the twins. Luke's heart warmed at the sight. If he closed his eyes, he could picture the same scene with Riley, only he hoped there would only be one child in her arms. He wanted many, but one at a time seemed more doable.

Her being a twin meant it ran in families, but he'd always heard it skipped a generation.

"I should get over to the studio and work," she said.

She'd only taken a sip of her wine, which he knew meant she'd planned on pulling an all-nighter.

"Can't you stay for a few minutes? We're celebrating the birth of two new Aspen Cove residents."

At the mention of her leaving, Bowie chimed in, "You can't go now, all the girls are on their way. Maisey is heading to our house to watch Sahara and Sage and Lydia are on their way."

Doc piped in, "Even Agatha is coming, and she doesn't miss *The Bachelor* for anyone."

They all laughed at that.

Luke looked at her pleadingly. "Take tonight off. I promise to help in any way I can."

She caved into the pressure easily, picked up her glass, and took a deep drink.

"You're a bad influence, Luke Mosier."

"No risk, no reward."

She leaned into him and purred, "Is there a reward?"

He bit his lip and shook his head. "Oh baby, I'll show you when we get home."

He felt her body shudder next to his. It was exactly what

he wanted more of later, only when she shuddered next time, they'd be naked, and he'd be deep inside her.

A few minutes later, Sage and Lydia walked in, followed by Samantha and Dalton.

The girls squealed with delight. They took out their phones and showed off pictures of the twins as if they'd given birth to them themselves.

Agatha walked in, all smiles. "I'm a grandma," she announced.

The guys pulled several tables together in the center of the room. What had been an intimate gathering turned into a party. Even Tilden joined them.

Several glasses of wine later, Sage stood up and made an announcement. "Seeing those babies made me want one." Her eyes went to Cannon. "What do you say? You want to knock me up?"

His eyes got wide, and his mouth dropped open. "Now?"

She sidled up to him and whispered in his ear.

Cannon raced behind the bar. When he returned, he tossed his brother Bowie the keys and swept Sage into his arms. "Have a good night, all. I've got a job to do."

As soon as the door closed behind them, the remaining crowd broke into laughter.

Bowie turned to Sage's sister Lydia, who was also one of the town's doctors. "What about you? Are you next?"

She shook her head. "I'm still trying to raise Wes."

Doc grumbled something about youth being wasted on the young. "Where is that man of yours?"

"He's in Frazier Falls this week with Noah Lockhart.

They're checking out some kind of sustainable house building project a guy named Owen Cooper has developed."

"I'm putting one of their houses on my property," Luke said.

All eyes turned to him.

"Where did you finally buy?" Bowie asked. "I heard you were looking at the property next to Abby Garrett."

The only people who knew about his purchase were Doc, Samantha, Dalton, Riley, and Thomas. He wasn't much of a talker and tended to keep information close to his chest. It was a surprise even to him that he'd talked of his love for Riley in front of Cannon.

"I bought the lot next to Dalton and Samantha's." He took a drink of his wine. "I was looking at property next to Abby's, but it's in a sealed trust and can't be purchased. The land has changed hands several times. It belonged to the Coolidge family, and then the Carvers. The last owner was Bea Bennett, but then it was turned over to a lawyer and is now in a trust."

"Fine purchase, son. You'll be happy there." Doc shook his head. "That Bea had her hands in a lot of things. It wouldn't surprise me if another pink letter showed up down the road."

Everyone looked at Doc, because if anyone knew about Bea's pink letters, it was him. He'd delivered the bulk of them the day of her funeral.

"You know something, don't you?" Katie asked. She'd been a recipient of one of Bea's pink letters. It was what brought her to Aspen Cove.

Doc drained his beer. "I know a lot of things. Right now, I know I need to go to bed, or I'll be grumpy in the morning."

Lydia laughed. "You're grumpy every morning." She'd been working with him for almost a year now, after coming to Aspen Cove to stay and help out until she found her dream job. Little did she know, she'd not only get a job, she'd find a husband, too.

"Are you ready, Lovey?" Doc asked Agatha. "I DVR'd your show."

She wrapped her arm through his. "You're such a romantic."

Luke emptied his wine glass. "I think we're out, too." He turned to her. "Ready to go?" He offered his hand and helped her up. "Got to get this one to bed."

Bowie laughed. "You mean get that one in bed. All this talk of love and babies and everything."

Dalton put his hands over his ears. "Dude, that's my cousin. I don't want the details."

Luke congratulated Trig once more and guided Riley to his SUV. "I'll drop you off at the diner in the morning."

She narrowed her eyes. "You're making sure I can't leave in the middle of the night."

"That, too. I want to wake up with you next to me." Leaving her car at her apartment was a good plan. She'd be less likely to abandon his bed in the middle of the night if she had to walk several blocks in the cold mountain air. Even in late summer, the day temperatures could drop fifty degrees by nightfall.

Once they were at his home, he took her straight to bed.

He didn't hurry but took his time to show her how much he loved her. Words were just words, but actions were concrete. He stroked her body until she quivered beneath him. Soon after, he found his own pleasure.

Side by side, they faced each other. He thumbed her chin so she would look at him.

"I meant every word I said."

Her lazy, sated smile made him happy. "What part?"

He kissed her forehead. "All the parts." He kissed the tip of her nose. "The one you should focus on is I love you." He kissed her lips.

She gave in to him so easily, her mouth opened, and their tongues danced together. When he pulled away, he saw a tear slide down her cheek.

"I know it's soon, but it's real." He touched his heart. "I've never said those words to anyone but my family and my horse."

Her eyes grew wide. "I'm up there with your horse?"

He laughed. "Baby, you're up there above everyone, including my horse—who, by the way, bucked me off and left me stranded several miles from home."

"What did you do?"

He decided to mess with her. "Sold him to a company that makes dog food."

She gasped. "You did not."

He shook his head. "No, I didn't. My father took him to Wyoming, where he spent his final days eating his way through several acres of grass."

"You're a good man, Luke Mosier." She placed her hand

over his heart. "I've never been told by a man that he loved me. I'm not sure how it's supposed to feel, but it feels right. It makes me feel warm inside, but it also scares the hell out of me." She snuggled closer to him. So close he could no longer see her eyes. "I love you, too. I may have loved you that first day at the diner when I saw your green eyes."

"Then I was mean to you."

She nodded against his chest. "Yes, you were, but you've more than made up for that."

"And you're still scared?" He splayed his hands across her back and pulled her to him so they were skin to skin. He wanted to assure her that he was nothing to fear.

"Loving someone this much is risky. What if I wake up one morning and it's all gone? How will I survive?"

Her life experiences didn't lend themselves to high levels of trust. It was a shame he'd have to redeem all of her past relationships through his actions, but he would.

"I'll never leave you, Riley. I won't turn my back on you when you need me. I'm here for you, always."

"You better be, or you'll find yourself sent out to pasture like your horse."

CHAPTER TWENTY-FIVE

The next few days passed by in a blur of pancakes, steel guitars, and love.

Riley delivered Doc's breakfast and asked how things were going.

"I woke up, so that's a pretty good start for a man my age."

She wanted to ask how old that was but knew it would be rude. Her best guess was early seventies, but he could have been ninety for all she knew.

He looked around the diner. There were a few regulars, but it was slow. "Have a seat, young lady. You look like you're about to drop."

She'd been putting in a lot of hours the last few days. If she averaged four hours of sleep a night, she'd be surprised. She slid into the booth across from him.

"You need something from me, Doc?"

He took a bite of pancake and chewed, but it seemed to Riley he was chewing on more than food.

"I wanted to get to know you better. Tell me what you love."

The first thought that came to mind was Luke, and she had no doubt Doc knew her exact thought by her blush.

"I mean outside of that fine young man of yours." He sipped his coffee. A brown stain formed on his white mustache until he wiped it dry.

"I'm finding my way. I like working here. It makes me feel like I'm part of something. As you know, I'm an artist." She sat taller as she said the words. "I love working with metal."

"What about your family?"

She felt a squeeze to her heart thinking about her father and brother. Thinking about Kathy always left her cold.

"I've got a twin."

He swallowed the bite in his mouth. "Seems to be a plague around here. All these things are coming in twos."

"There's only your grandsons that I know of, right?"

He tipped his head from side to side. "Yep, Jason and Jonah, you and your brother, and there's the two Lockharts."

"Oh, wow, it's not often you run into so many twins. I'm obviously not identical to Baxter. What about the Lockharts? Are they identical twins like your grandsons?"

"Oh no, Quinn is as fair as a Nordic, and Bayden is his polar opposite."

She thought back to the day she'd met Noah Lockhart and seen him leave with three men. There was a blonde in the group she never considered would be related to them.

"Baxter and I have a similar look, but he's taller, and of course, he's a man."

"Are you two close?"

"Geography puts a damper on things. He's in Boise, and I'm here, but we love each other."

Doc pushed his plate to the side. He leaned back against the red pleather booth and crossed his hands in front of him, placing them gently on the table. She'd heard from the guys that he had a stance and a phrase that was a precursor to a lesson, but she doubted he'd say, "Now listen here, son" to her.

"I'm gonna give you some words of wisdom, because I think of all you youngsters as my kin. Don't let miles separate you. Don't let words become walls. I lost my daughter for ten years because we were both afraid of losing each other, and the funny thing was, ten years of silence was exactly that. Don't let ten years go by. Don't let unsettled business fester in your heart."

She wondered if he had a spyglass into her soul. She'd been thinking about her brother. Thinking about her father and all the words she would have liked to have said to him. The most important being she loved him. There were many words she'd saved for Kathy, but after talking to Luke, she wasn't sure those words were appropriate anymore. Maybe the only word she had for her stepmother was, why?

"You know, you're right. I think I'm going to take my break and call my brother." She picked up Doc's empty plate and bent over to kiss him on the cheek. "Thanks for the talk, Doc."

"Anytime, Riley. Age gives you wisdom and hemorrhoids, and only one of those is something I'd pass on."

"Thankfully." She buzzed past Meg and told her she was taking ten. Walking through the kitchen, she grabbed her cell phone and headed out back.

It was a beautiful late summer day. The birds sang, and the wind moved the scent of pine through the air.

She sat on the step behind the diner and dialed her brother.

"Hey, Rye," he said in his baritone voice. Even when he was a boy, no one expected that deep, dark, honeyed tone to come out of his mouth. "How's Mayberry RFD?"

He'd teased her about moving to the small town. Told her she'd be bored in ten minutes and move back to Butte.

"I love it here." She explained to him about the benefits of knowing everyone and how she'd finished up the two sculptures at four that morning.

"I was joking about living in Mayberry, but maybe I wasn't too far off the mark."

She laughed. It felt good to laugh with her brother since the last couple of times they talked, all she had left were tears.

"It's better than that because it's real. I'm telling you, my life has come full circle. Between the job, having family here, the studio and Luke, I'm in heaven. What about you?"

Baxter sighed loudly into the phone. "Full circle hasn't hit me yet. I'm still wandering on a long stretch of nothingness."

"You can always come to Aspen Cove. There seems to be a lot of building going on, and maybe you could find a position. There's a contractor here named Wes Covington. He'd be a great contact for you."

"I'll keep that in mind." In the background, someone called for him. "Got to go, sis."

"Right." Saying goodbye was the hardest thing to do. She seemed to be doing that a lot this last year, but things were changing, and maybe she'd convince her brother to come along for the ride. "Just wanted to call and tell you I love you."

Baxter returned the sentiment.

As she returned to her shift, a feeling of calm washed over her. Doc was right, family was important, and she vowed not to let the miles separate her from those she loved.

When she walked up to the back counter, she noticed Meg had done all of her side work while she'd been on her break. She'd gone out of her way to be nice. Riley wasn't questioning her motives because she didn't want to borrow trouble. Meg had taken a turn since their heart-to-heart last week. It was far better to have her as a friend than an enemy.

"You working at the studio tonight?" Meg filled up the last sugar jar and placed it on the brown plastic tray. Riley followed her out, and they both went about placing them on nearby tables.

"The sculptures are finished, but I have to go in for about an hour to clean up. Luke is bringing his crew in tomorrow morning to pick up the work and deliver it to the stage."

"That would be a sight to see. A bunch of hulking firemen flexing their muscles."

Riley didn't want to say she saw that every night when

Luke raised himself over her and pressed into her waiting body.

"Those suckers are heavy. I attached wheels so they'd be easier to move, but there was nothing I could do to make the move from the studio to the stage simple."

Meg looked around the diner. "Sure is slow in here. How am I supposed to keep myself in cigarettes and wine if people don't eat?"

"Most of the male population are making sure the venue is ready for the masses that will show up next week for the concert."

"I love the word mass. Makes me think naughty thoughts."

Riley laughed. "Makes me think about confession."

"If you want to go and get your studio stuff done, I can hold down the fort. If the masses show up early, I'll give you a call."

Grateful to have the afternoon off, Riley grabbed her purse and left. It wasn't as if staying would make a difference. Zero customers meant zero tips. Her time was better spent cleaning up and preparing for other things—like a romantic night with Luke.

She left work feeling good but nervous. She texted Samantha and told her she could take a peek at the finished product in an hour.

The concert would be the first time her work would be on display. After the show, Samantha wanted to put the sculptures in the gallery. She was certain they'd bring a good price. Riley's stomach churned with the thought that people might hate her work. What if Kathy was right? What if her passion for metal art turned out to be worthless?

Samantha showed up as Riley scooped the last bit of dust into the trash can. She watched her face for any sign of disappointment, but there was none. Samantha seemed to love everything about them, but old hurts were hard to bury. Each time she heard Samantha compliment her, she also heard Kathy's voice in the back of her head criticize her. Her doubts and fears resurfaced. The best cure to banish those was time with Luke.

CHAPTER TWENTY-SIX

Luke's phone rang, and a smile spread across his face.

"Hey, beautiful. What are you doing?"

"Hey, yourself. I'm closing up shop for the day and heading to your place."

He could hear the exhaustion in her voice. She'd been burning the candle at both ends and no doubt needed to sleep for a week straight.

"Why don't you climb in bed and get some rest while I finish up my shift?"

"Mmm, that sounds good. Will you wake me when you get home?"

He loved the way she said 'home,' as if she'd finally decided to move in with him. While they hadn't discussed it again since his first offer, he did plan to revisit the question tomorrow once the sculptures were in place and her schedule was calmer.

"How do you want me to wake you?" He loved to tease her. Closing his eyes, he could imagine the blush rising to her cheeks. "You want me to kiss you awake, or should I slide next to your naked body and do naughty things to you until you wake up?"

He heard a cough coming from the direction of his office door. Thomas stood there making obscene gestures with his hands and mouth until Luke flew him the bird and motioned for him to shut the door.

"I'd like both," she said. "I want your soft kisses and hard body."

He shifted uncomfortably in his seat. All she had to do was say the word 'hard,' and he was.

"Go climb into bed, and I'll see you after my shift." He wouldn't get off work until late that night, but now he had something to look forward to. "And Riley?"

"Yeah?"

"I love you, and when I get home, I'll show you how much."

She giggled. It was a sweet sound that hugged him like a warm blanket.

"Love you, too."

He walked out of his office and into Thomas, who was waiting by the door.

"You're so whipped."

"Guilty." Luke wouldn't deny it. He was unequivocally smitten with Riley. They were opposite in almost every way, but it was like their individualized pieces somehow fit together perfectly. Where he was regimented, she was undisciplined. Where he was tall, she was petite. He was dark, and she was light. She filled all the empty spaces inside him, and he hoped he did the same for her.

"I can't believe you're giving in so damn easily. Pretty soon, she'll have your dick in her hand like a leash."

"God, I hope so. You should be so lucky to have yours in some beautiful woman's hand."

Thomas tapped his chest with his fist. "Confirmed bachelor."

"How is living in that house all by yourself?" Thomas had closed on his new place a few days prior.

"Heaven, man. It's like having a castle and I'm the king."

"Tell yourself that now, but soon you'll see how quiet that place will be and how those walls become a moat separating you from the world."

Luke thought about his life and counted himself lucky he'd finally gotten everything he wanted. He had the perfect job, a woman who loved him, and a community that had become his family.

James showed up with his arms full. "Look what Poppy brought by." His right hand held out a calendar with February showing.

"Look at loverboy wearing a rose and a puppy."

"Give me that." Luke swiped it from his hand and stared at the picture. He had to admit the puppy was cute.

Thomas took a copy from James and flipped to his month. "Damn, I'm hot."

Luke turned to June to see Thomas's shot and laughed. Charlie had brought over a Saint Bernard puppy to pose with him. In the background, she'd Photoshopped in a bursting fire hydrant. Both Thomas and the puppy were soaked.

James held the calendar out and shook his head. "I don't see hot. All I see is a washed-up old man."

"You better watch it, or you'll be doing my laundry again."

James frowned. "You need a wife or a housekeeper."

"Why?" Thomas asked. "I've got you, and you don't require anything of me."

IT WAS CLOSING in on eight o'clock when an alarm went off in the Guild Center. Luke's first reaction was to think Riley hadn't gone home but stayed to work on something else. The grid was lit on her studio, which meant she had to be there and hadn't turned on the exhaust system.

"You want to go, or do you want the whole team?"

He considered going on his own, but his crew hadn't done a drill this week, so to keep them on their toes, he told them all to gear up. Less than three minutes later, they were in the rig with sirens wailing, speeding down Main Street toward the alarm.

Luke expected to see nothing, but what greeted him was a surprise.

Black smoke rose into the air and billowed into the darkening sky. The building screamed with alarms as if crying because of injury. His crew kicked into gear.

They raced around back to the closest entry point to

Riley's studio. He searched the parking lot for her beat-up SUV, but it wasn't there. He was a mix of emotions. Thrilled and relieved she wasn't there, and angry she'd left something unattended and put others at risk. He knew she'd been too tired to work so many hours. Knew she'd get sloppy and make a mistake. He never considered it would send the center up in flames.

They hooked up the hose and went to work. Between the state-of-the-art safety system Samantha had installed and his crew's expertise, the fire was under control in less than an hour. Fortunately for everyone, it was contained to Riley's studio and some water damage to the hallway and Cannon's studio.

In the middle of the heap of charred ruins stood the sculptures. The beautiful patina Riley had worked so hard to create was now black with soot and grime, but to her credit, the metalworks were still intact. Even the heat of the blazing fire hadn't compromised her art.

"Accidental?" Thomas asked.

Luke spun toward his friend. "Of course. Do you think she'd set the place on fire on purpose?"

"No, but we have to investigate all possibilities." He looked past Luke to the remains.

All the men had their place on the team. Luke was the man in charge. For all intents and purposes, the fire chief. Thomas fell into second-in-command. He had several jobs, one of which was as the fire department's investigator. James was trained for EMS, and Jacob was the driver and all around go-to. The part-timers filled in the blanks where needed.

"She didn't set the fire on purpose, Thomas." He hated that he wasn't being open-minded about the possibilities, but this was Riley they were talking about, and his love for her was skewing his common sense.

"You need to step away from this or step away from her while we investigate."

"What?"

"On first inspection, it's not looking good for her." He pointed to the wall where she usually kept the tanks, but one was pulled forward and left in the center of the room. The rubber tubing that delivered the gas was melted into the cement floor. The blanket they'd made love on was charred to ash in the corner. The shelving lay twisted and mangled, its joints and fasteners not able to take the concentration of heat.

Above them was the only place the ceiling had given way to the fire. Thankfully, it hadn't breached the room, or the whole place might have gone up in flames. As it was, there would be smoke damage throughout the building and water damage to areas close by.

"She didn't set the fire."

Luke knew without a doubt she didn't set it intentionally, but he couldn't be certain she hadn't set it accidentally.

"You can't be objective."

"I have to be. I'm in charge of this station, and it's my job to protect this town."

"You're also Riley's boyfriend, and you have some obligation to protect her. Where do you draw the line for either?"

He saw where Thomas was going, but he had a job to do. He'd promised to serve and protect.

They taped off the area and called Samantha and Dalton, who came right away.

While Samantha tried to remain stoic and unaffected, he saw the concern in her eyes.

"We're insured," she said. "It will be okay."

"Does Riley know?" Dalton asked.

Thomas gave him a look. He was certain it was a reminder of how impossible being objective would be.

Luke shook his head. "No, she's not the owner of the building, but I will visit her and let her know." The next sentence would be hard to say. "We can't rule out arson, and she's a suspect."

A tiny gasp cleared Samantha's lips. "You think she set the place on fire." She shook her head so hard, her hair swirled around her shoulders like a building tornado. "No way. I was here earlier. She was so excited to finish the sculptures."

"Did she look tired?" Thomas asked.

"Exhausted, but..." Samantha's head fell forward. "I suppose she could have accidentally started it." She looked around. "I'm having a tough time believing that, too. The place was immaculate. She was scooping up the last bit of trash into the dust bin when I arrived. There wasn't a thing out of place."

Even though Luke had accused her of being irresponsible the first day they met, he'd seen nothing that could confirm his initial suspicions. Riley was a safety-first girl. Short of almost burning the diner down because of the temperamental toaster, he'd seen nothing to give him the impression she'd been careless in any facet of her life.

Luke looked to Thomas. "Ready to pack it up?" He walked toward the rig, with Samantha and Dalton close behind. Before he climbed on, he said, "I'll notify Riley."

On the way back to the station, he considered the easiest way to break his love's heart.

CHAPTER TWENTY-SEVEN

Riley woke when the bed dipped beside her, and the smell of smoke filled her nostrils. She'd been in a dead sleep for hours. Once the guitar pieces were complete, the stress of the project fell away and her ability to let go and finally succumb to the exhaustion hit her. She felt like she could sleep for a week.

"Hey, you're home. What time is it?"

She had a hard time focusing on him. The room was dark but for a slice of moonlight that bled through the crack in the curtain.

"It's time for you to get up."

She rubbed her eyes. "Really? I thought you were going to come to bed and do naughty things to my body."

He pulled the cover and rubbed his hand over her back. His fingers traced the grid of scars on her back.

"That was the plan, but not anymore. Something has happened, and I need you to get up and get dressed."

She bolted up to a seated position. She couldn't ignore the serious tone of his voice, and once again the smell of smoke wafted beneath her nose.

"A fire?"

Her eyes had adjusted enough to see the pained expression on his face.

"Yes."

Her hand went to her mouth. "Oh my God. Is anyone hurt? Is it Aunt Maisey, Dalton and Samantha, Sage?" She recited all the names of the townspeople she knew, but he kept shaking his head. "Who the hell is hurt, then?"

"No one, but the Guild Creative Center nearly burned down, and the fire started in your studio."

"What? No..." She couldn't believe she'd heard him correctly. "That's not possible."

"It happened, Riley. I'm not making it up."

"What does that mean? Is the building gone? What about everyone's work? What about my work?"

"Your studio is the only one directly affected by actual fire. There's smoke damage and water damage, but it's minimal."

She climbed out of bed and threw on her clothes. "I need to go see." She tugged on her socks and shoes, hopping all the way to the living room.

"You can't. You can't go anywhere near there. What I need you to do is go back to your apartment. The sheriff will stop by to take your statement."

"My statement?" She spun around and looked at him. "You think I started the fire?"

"I'm not at liberty to discuss anything pertaining to an ongoing investigation."

A lump caught in her throat and tears sprung to her eyes, as if she'd stood in the center of the acrid smoke.

"You're kicking me out?"

His head nodded before his words came out. "I can't investigate the fire if I'm sleeping with the number one suspect."

He looked pained, but his look was nothing compared to the pain in her chest.

"I didn't start that fire." She thought back to the night and knew she couldn't have started anything. She'd never used her equipment. The only thing she touched was the broom and dustpan. "You have to believe me."

He picked up her purse and handed it to her. "I have to do my job, and until the investigation is finished, we can't be together."

Riley's immediate reaction was to fall to her knees and beg him, but she knew better. The look in his eyes reminded her of all the looks she'd received in her life. Somehow, her word wasn't good enough. Never good enough.

She climbed in her SUV and headed back to her apartment. It was well after dark, and she had the early shift at the diner.

She slogged up the stairs, kicked off her shoes and climbed into bed fully dressed. She cried for all the injustices of the world. She cried for the homeless, the poor, the abused, but most of all she cried because once again she was alone in the world.

———

WHEN HER ALARM WENT OFF, she dragged herself out of bed. Every muscle in her body ached. One look in the mirror told her no amount of makeup would hide the dark circles and bags under her eyes.

She'd tossed and turned all night. She'd dreamed of smoke and fire and destruction. The scars on her back ached at the memory. Her heart became an eviscerated, empty organ.

Each time she closed her eyes, she saw Luke and his look of pain. Somehow, what looked like loss last night morphed into a look of validation inside her mind. Like somehow what he thought of her initially had come true.

She did her best to make herself presentable and walked across the street to the diner.

Meg was already there, hunched over the back counter. She looked over her shoulder.

"You look like shit."

"I feel worse than I look."

Smoke rose from the toaster, and Meg let out a howl. Immediately, she rushed to the sink and ran her hand under ice cold water. "Damn toaster. Did you spin the dial again before you left yesterday?"

"I left before you." Riley threw her purse in the back

room and rushed out to get a clean bar-towel and ice. "Let me see that."

"It's bad." She moved her hand from under the running water.

Riley gasped at the fully formed blister. "Damn, I've never seen anything blister so quickly."

"It hurts like a mother."

"Let me get the first aid kit."

Inside were burn cream and bandages. Riley fixed up her friend's hand and told her to take a seat while she waited on the early birds.

She moved around the restaurant pouring coffee and listening to whispers about the fire. She knew they were pointing fingers at her, but what could she say? She felt like she'd been set up from the beginning to take a fall. First, it was Luke, who'd basically told the world she was stupid and irresponsible with the gas tanks in her car.

Then it was Meg, who accused her of trying to burn down the diner and perpetuated the 'Riley is a firebug' rumor. Now her studio had caught fire, so she didn't have much room to defend herself.

"You set the center on fire. Why did you do it?" Meg asked as Riley approached the counter.

"Oh my God, you, too?"

She lifted her shoulders in an exaggerated shrug. "What am I supposed to think? It's all the buzz around town."

Riley tossed her towel to the counter. "I came here for a fresh start. I was seeking a place where I could be me. Where no one would judge me." Her voice rose enough that people

226

turned to look at her. "I thought I'd found my place. Somewhere I belonged." She reached inside the swinging doors and grabbed her purse. She glanced at Ben cooking. "Tell Aunt Maisey thank you for everything, but it's not going to work out."

She stopped in front of Meg. "Because people say something doesn't make it true. Everyone in town says awful things about you, but I made up my own mind. Turns out maybe my stepmother was right. She always said I had no sense." She shrugged her purse to her shoulder and marched to the door. Before she opened it, she turned around and looked at everyone in the diner. In the corner sat Doc and Agatha. Tilden Cool sat at the counter opposite Meg. A few tourists and some locals she wasn't on a first name basis with filled the other booths and tables. "As a statement of public record, I didn't start the Guild Center on fire." She swung the door open and walked right into Sheriff Cooper.

"I was coming to see you," he said.

Riley gritted her teeth so hard, she was sure her molars would crack. "You want to put me in cuffs?"

Sheriff Aiden Cooper's head snapped back like she'd slapped him. "No, I was coming to get your statement. Do I have a reason to put you in cuffs?"

Doc somehow made his way to her without her noticing.

"Now, listen here," he said in his fatherly manner. "No one is going out of here in cuffs."

He gave the sheriff a hard look. "Aiden, the girl's been through enough. The whole damn town has tried and convicted her, and we both know she's not guilty of setting the fire on purpose."

Riley suppressed a growl. "I didn't set the fire on purpose or accidentally." She pushed past the sheriff and walked across the street to his office. If he wanted to lock her up, fine.

"Riley, wait up," the sheriff called after her.

"You don't need to cuff me or Taser me, Sheriff. I've got no fight left in me."

He caught up with her. "I don't think you started the fire, but I need your statement."

"You don't?" It was the first spark of hope she had.

"No, and neither does Luke, but you have to understand he has a job to do. If he took your side, he would lose credibility."

A stabbing pain pierced her heart. "It's okay, Sheriff, you don't need to defend him. I know he's doing his job, but Jeez, for once in my life, it would have been nice to have someone choose me."

She followed him into the station, where Mark Bancroft sat at his desk and Poppy Bancroft sat at hers. Behind her hung the beefcake calendar. She'd turned it to April of next year, which happened to be Mark's month.

"Come on in and have a seat." Sheriff Cooper pointed to the chair in front of his desk. He turned to Poppy and Mark. "I'd love a muffin and a coffee from the bakery."

They hopped up and vacated the room.

"You didn't have to kick them out. I don't have anything to confess." She saw the calendar on his desk. "Can I look at that?"

He slid it to her. She flipped from the back forward. December gave her a giggle despite the somber situation. Seeing Doc in a Santa suit with candy cane boxers and knee-high red and white striped socks was humorous. She flipped through the pages until she came to February, and her heart did a triple twisting somersault into the pit of her stomach.

"How come the ones you love hurt you the most?" She closed the calendar and put it back on his desk.

"It hurts because you love them."

She set her hands on her lap and looked up with teary eyes. She fought to keep her emotions in check.

"What did you want to ask me, Sheriff?"

He took her statement. All she could tell him was she'd cleaned up the shop and walked out the back door. She hadn't used any equipment that day that could start a fire. Her tanks were stored next to the wall. The spares she had were stored in the warehouse.

"What about the propane torch you use for smaller items?"

"It was on the workbench. I haven't used it since I arrived. I've had no need for it." She thought it odd he'd asked about it, but then again, she knew he would need to be thorough. There would be an investigation for insurance purposes, as well as criminal negligence.

He finished his notes and smiled. "You're free to go."

"Am I? Do I need to stay in town?"

His brows lifted. "You planning on leaving?"

She nodded. "I learned long ago to listen to my gut, and it says I'm not welcome here."

He shook his head. "I learned long ago to listen to my heart. It's a far better gauge." The chair legs scraped against the cement floor when he pushed, lifted from his chair, and walked around his desk. "You're not under arrest, Riley, but I think you should stay around. You'd be surprised at what people are saying about you."

She looked over her shoulder to the diner. "Oh, I've heard the whispers."

"Then you haven't been listening." He walked her to the door. "Are you hearing what people are truly saying, or are you hearing what you expect them to say?"

She walked out of the office, wondering for the second time since she'd lived in Aspen Cove if she was losing her mind. Weeks ago, Luke had asked her something similar. Was she simply misinterpreting people's actions?

She thought back to what she'd said to Meg; because people said one thing didn't make it so. She had a lot to think about. Mainly what her next plan was. Maybe she'd be heading to Boise to see Baxter.

She walked at a snail's pace to her apartment. As soon as she opened the back door, she was greeted by Katie and a hug.

"You okay?"

"Sure, I'm being accused of being an arsonist. Life sure isn't dull in Aspen Cove."

"I know you didn't set that fire. No one else that matters believes it."

"Meg thinks I did. She basically announced it to everyone within earshot of the diner."

"Meg doesn't matter."

Katie pulled her into the back of the bakery and plucked several muffins, brownies, and cookies from cooling trays and plated them.

"You look exhausted. Take this upstairs and rest. It will all work out."

She gave her friend a hug and walked upstairs with the goodies. It would all work out as soon as she could pack up her stuff and be gone.

CHAPTER TWENTY-EIGHT

Luke hated he had to push Riley away, but he needed to separate himself from his relationship so he could do his job.
Without his paycheck, he couldn't move forward with the
relationship he wanted to have with her.

He knew she was a safety-first woman. He'd watched her
in action this past month. Something didn't sit right with the
fire; he felt it in his gut, but he had to entertain the possibility
that Riley had inadvertently left the flame going. She did say
she was exhausted.

"I'm heading to the center to look around again," Thomas
said.

Luke pushed his chair from his desk. "I'll go with you."

"Nope."

"What do you mean no?"

"Think about it. Think long and hard about where you
need to be. I'm an asshole when it comes to women, but

you're worse. She needs you, man. Your job will be here. No one can fire you but Samantha, and you know she's not going to do that. Make the right choice. I've got this. It's what I do."

Luke's gut ached when Thomas mentioned choice, because he knew he'd screwed up. All Riley ever wanted was to be someone's choice, and he'd let her down.

"I'm such an idiot."

"Been telling you that for months."

"This time, you're right."

Luke took off from the station at a run. He sprinted up the block to the back side of the bakery. When he got there, he rang the bell several times, but no one answered. He pounded on the back door until Katie answered.

"Have you seen Riley?" His voice was heavy with desperation.

Katie looked up the stairs. "Did you ring her bell?"

He nodded. "She didn't answer."

"Maybe she's resting. She's been through a lot."

He knew she'd been through hell, and it was his responsibility to guide her back.

"I know, and I wasn't there for her, but I want to be."

Katie let out a heavy sigh. "How men have made it to the twenty-first century is a mystery to me." She pointed up the stairs. "I can let you in this door, but she'll have to let you in the next one."

Luke rushed up the stairs and knocked. He waited a few minutes and knocked again.

"Who is it?" Riley's voice asked.

She knew it was him because he could see her shadow through the peephole.

"It's Luke. Let me in."

"Flowers and lots of groveling might work." Katie went back into the bakery to leave him alone with the voice behind the door.

"What do you want?"

He wanted a lot of things, but mostly right now he wanted to hold her. "I want you. I choose you, Riley. I'm sorry I didn't put you first."

"What about your job?"

"This isn't about my job, it's about us."

He could hear her whimpers through the wood.

"There is no us."

"Open the door, Riley, and I'll prove you wrong. The only thing that matters is us. I'll sit on the step in front of your door until you do."

He listened to the chain fall and the lock disengage. When she cracked open the door, he pushed it wider and pulled her into his arms.

"God, I'm sorry. I'm such an idiot. Loving you means putting you first, and I'm sorry I lost sight of what was important for a second. It took a bigger idiot to remind me of that."

"Who?" She swiped at her tears and moved inside to where she'd been packing the milk crate full of her things. On top was the erector set she'd prized all her life.

"Thomas."

She sniffled. "He told you to come here?"

"No, but he told me I was an asshole."

She nodded. "Yes, you were."

He pulled the erector set from the box and set it back on the shelf.

She picked it up and put it back in the box.

"What are you doing?"

"I'm packing."

He glanced around and found her suitcase by the door. His throat turned dry. Ten minutes later, and she would have been gone.

"You were going to leave me without saying goodbye?"

She inhaled a shaky breath. "I was preparing to leave. I hadn't made a solid plan yet."

He pulled her into his arms. "Riley, you can't leave me. I'm less without you."

"You're employed without me."

"What's the point of a job if I don't have someone to talk to about it?"

She pressed her head into his chest. "It will pay for your fancy new house on the lake."

"A house that will be missing its heart if you're not there."

She burst into tears. "I didn't start the fire."

"I know you didn't, but someone did, and we have to figure it out."

"You should go, then. I don't want anyone talking badly about you. I'm bad for you."

He lifted her chin. "You're the only thing that's good for me. Thomas is investigating and he'll figure it out."

"What if he doesn't? I can't stay here and have people whispering behind my back. No way I could live in a place where everyone thought I was guilty but got off because my boyfriend is the fire chief."

He understood where she was coming from. He wouldn't want to live with a cloud of doubt hovering above his head either.

He led her to the sofa and sat down, tugging her into his lap. "It will be okay. I know it here"—he touched his stomach—"and here." He touched his heart.

"You pushed me away."

"We've already established I'm an idiot."

She curled into his lap, and he held her until she fell asleep.

Throughout the rest of the day, he exchanged texts with Thomas, who had found some clues he believed exonerated Riley, but he was tight-lipped about the details. All he would say was to meet him in the diner the next day, and to bring her.

When the sun set and dark of night blanketed the town, Luke took her to bed. While he would have loved to have made love to her, that's not what she needed. She needed to know he was there for her through thick and thin. Even though he needed a nudge, he chose her above all else. It was the right thing to do. The only thing to do.

―――――

"WHY DO I have to go with you?" Riley shrugged on a T-shirt and tucked it into her jeans.

"I don't know. Thomas asked both of us to be there."

"People will stare at me."

"Yes, but because you're beautiful."

"They'll stare at you, too."

He walked toward her with a swagger in his step. "Because I look like a troll and they want to know how I got so lucky."

"Right." She gave him an exaggerated eye-roll. "More likely because you're hanging out with the town riff-raff."

He grabbed her by the waist and pulled her to him. "Once this is behind us, we're going to have to work on your self-esteem problems. You had no problem standing your ground the day I met you. Why be a shrinking violet now?"

"I had nothing to lose the day I met you. I was trying on a new personality, so there was no risk."

He laughed because she was adorable. Especially the way her hands tentatively touched his hips and then moved with confidence around to grip the globes of his ass.

"You weren't trying on a new personality, you were letting yours go free. Your stepmother did a real job on reining you in. I bet it was because deep inside she knew you'd be a force to be reckoned with if you were ever allowed to use your voice."

She stood taller and lifted her chin. "You think?"

He brushed his lips against hers. "I know, baby. I know." He deepened the kiss until her fingers moved up to his back and dug into his muscles.

As much as he wanted to continue, he couldn't. They needed to be at the diner. "Can I have a rain check?"

She moved her body against his, causing the exact reaction she expected, the one he didn't need if he had to be seen in public.

"You'd rather go to the diner than to bed?"

He leaned forward and nipped at her lip. "I'd much rather be in bed with you naked, but something tells me this is important. Thomas has sent me two reminders this morning."

She stepped back. "What if they cuff me and take me away?"

The laugh started low in his stomach and worked its way up until it came out in a thunderous volume.

"If they were going to take you in, they'd simply come here and knock on the door."

He hadn't realized she was holding her breath until she let it loose and her body deflated in front of him.

"Okay, then, I'm ready."

CHAPTER TWENTY-NINE

They entered the diner hand in hand.

Riley's heart raced like a horse at the Preakness. The beats were so loud, she swore hoofs pounded her ribcage.

Meg looked up from behind the front counter and rushed forward. "Thought you'd be in jail by now." She glanced down at their clasped hands and frowned. "Isn't she a problem for you?" She ignored Riley and looked straight at Luke.

He shook his head slowly. His hand moved to wrap around Riley's waist and tug her closer. "She's a problem, all right. Most men would be thrilled to have someone so diffi-cult." He leaned over and kissed her.

"You want a room or a table?"

Luke looked around and saw his corner booth still open. "We'll take my normal space." He led Riley to the booth and had her slide in first.

The bell above the door rang, and Thomas walked in, looking smug.

He slid into the booth across from Riley and Luke. "Hey, you two." He looked straight at Riley. "You look pale." He leaned in and stared at her. "Maybe with a hint of green."

She twisted her hands on top of the table. "I'm nervous."

"No need to be. Watch and learn." He lifted a coffee mug into the air and made eye contact with Meg.

She arrived several minutes later with a full pot.

"Hey, Thomas." She poured with her left hand, keeping her right tucked inside her pocket.

"Hey, love." He looked down at her left-handed pour and the mess she made of the table. "Practicing ambidexterity?"

"I find strength in both hands an asset." After a suggestive wink, she poured the rest of the table coffee. She ignored Luke and Riley and kept her focus on Thomas. "Do you want or need anything else?"

He rolled his neck. "I'd die for a cigarette."

"You're easy."

Riley's head went back and forth between the two. She'd seen Meg in action, but today she was in fine form.

"But I'm not cheap," Thomas teased.

"I can hook you up." She glanced around the diner. "Be right back."

As soon as she was out of earshot, Luke chimed in. "What the hell are you doing? You don't smoke."

"I don't, and neither do you." He glanced at Riley. "Do you?"

"Nope."

"Pay attention," he told them both.

Meg pushed through the swinging doors with her purse in her hand. As if she was invited, she slid into the booth next to him and dug through her purse for a cigarette. "Here you go."

Thomas took the cigarette and placed it between his lips. It hung loose while he patted his pants pockets.

"Damn, forgot my lighter. You got one?" he asked Meg.

She looked down at her right hand, which sported a bandage on her index finger and thumb. She dug for one in her bag and came up empty-handed.

"I must have left my lighter at home."

Aiden Cooper entered the diner and pulled up a chair, pinning Meg in place.

"Where are we at in this thing?"

"This thing?" Meg asked. "What's this thing?"

Aiden's eyes focused on the bandages on Meg's hand. "You burn yourself?"

Meg's lips quivered before they turned up into a smile. "Yes, Riley was here." She pointed to the counter. "You know the toaster. It's always on the fritz."

Aiden looked at Riley. "Did you see her get burned?"

Riley cocked her head. "Yes." She shook her head. "No, I saw her yelp and then rush for the water but not the actual injury." Her eyes grew wide. "Oh my God." Riley covered her mouth with her hand. "Why?"

"Why what?" Meg asked, her face turning white.

Thomas let the cigarette drop to the table and reached into his pocket to pull out what was left of a lighter.

"Found this on the floor of Riley's studio." The plastic was melted into a puddle, except for the faint outline of a pinup girl. "Don't you have one like this, Meg?"

"I did, but..."

Aiden pulled his cuffs from his belt loop. "If you can produce yours, I'll let you go. If you can't, I'll have to take you in for questioning."

Meg's shoulders slumped forward. "Are you going to arrest me here in front of everyone?"

"Are you confessing to the crime?"

She looked around the table.

Riley asked the same question again. "Why?"

"Because you came into town and took everything away from me. I figured if you were gone, I had a chance of getting it back."

Luke fisted his hands until Riley set hers gently on top of his. "She took nothing away from you. You still had your job."

A tear slipped from Meg's face. "I didn't have you."

Luke moved out of the booth. "You never had me. You never would have. I'd been waiting for Riley all my life." He held out his hand. "You ready, sweetheart?"

She shook her head. "If she's leaving, I'll have to pull her shift."

Sheriff Cooper moved the cuffs to the table.

Riley scooted over and placed her hand on his forearm. "I know what it's like to be publicly humiliated. Can you spare her the embarrassment? If she gets up and walks out, can you arrest her outside?"

"Why do you care?" Thomas asked.

She shrugged. "Because I can't help it."

"You ready?" Sheriff Cooper asked. "We're going to get up and walk out the back."

Meg held back her tears and nodded. She rose from the booth and walked through the swinging doors.

"You're going to work her shift?"

She gave him a quick kiss. "Not for her, but for Aunt Maisey. I'll be home in a few hours."

"Home?"

She walked to the counter and pulled an apron from the shelf below. "Is that offer to move in still on the table?"

He looked around the diner before he sidled up next to her. "Are you saying yes?"

"Are you asking?"

He dropped down to his knees. "Riley Black, I love you, and I want you with me always. Will you come home to me?"

"Yes. I'll come home to you."

He swept her in his arms and swung her around. "She said yes."

"To shacking up," Doc said from his table. He rose and tossed a bill next to his empty plate. "You're worth more," Doc said to Riley before he shuffled toward the door.

"Don't you worry, Doc," Luke called after him. "She gets my heart first. The rest is a formality."

Doc waved them off before he left.

"You coming back to the station?" Thomas added. "We've got a report to write."

"Be right there." He rubbed noses with her. "You coming home right away?"

She pulled her lower lip between her teeth. "I've got something to take care of first."

He kissed her and stepped away. "See you soon, baby."

"Yes, you will," she whispered in his ear. "Will you be naked and in bed?"

"You're killing me."

"Yep, one stroke at a time."

AUNT MAISEY RUSHED through the door and pulled Riley in for a hug. "I'm so sorry. I had no idea."

"No need to be sorry. In the end, it all worked out."

Maisey tied her apron around her waist. "I hear you have a man waiting for you at home."

Riley laughed. "Are there no secrets?"

"Honey, you live in a small town. Gossip travels faster than the wind here." She cupped her face and gave her a motherly kiss. "Go to your man. Make peace. Make love. Make a life."

"I've got something to do first."

Aunt Maisey narrowed her eyes. "Something more important than finding your future?"

Riley smiled. "Yep, I'll never truly have a future if I can't let go of my past."

She picked up her purse and walked out the door. It was hard to believe yesterday she had packed up her belongings with the intent to run again. Hadn't her stepmother told her she was running from her past?

She climbed into her old car and started the engine. It purred to life on the first turn of the key. She had no idea where she was going. All she knew was, she needed a quiet place to think before she called Kathy.

She found herself at the old cemetery. As she meandered the path between the gravestones, she admired how beautiful and serene the grounds were.

A sparkle caught her eye. On the tombstone in front of her sat a tiny frame of a father, mother and a child. Her fingers traced the photo while her eyes scanned the names of the people buried there. Bill, Bea, and Brandy Bennett.

Over to the right sat a tall oak tree, its canopy spreading like a protective umbrella. Riley took a seat on the ground and pulled her phone from her bag. She stared at the screen. Could she confront the wounds of her past? Could she not? She raised and lowered her cell phone as she found the courage and lost it between breaths.

It seemed fitting to bury her past in a graveyard. She inhaled deeply and tapped out the numbers of the woman who raised her. On the third ring, Kathy answered.

"Riley? Is that you?"

"Hi." She'd always called her mom, but it didn't feel right at the moment.

"Are you okay?"

She leaned against the bark of the tree, letting the rough surface bite into her skin. "Yes, I'm great, but I'm calling to ask you why?"

"Why what?"

"Why did you hate me so much?"

She heard a shuffle and pictured Kathy pulling out her favorite skirted chair from the table. "I never hated you."

She gritted her teeth. It was hard not to lash out. Worse not to cry.

"What mother tells her daughter, even a stepdaughter, that she'd be pretty if she lost ten pounds, that her pursuits wouldn't garner anything but self-loathing and misery?"

There was a long pause before Kathy began. "I never hated you. I hated myself. I didn't want you to turn out like me. I married your dad so I'd have a place to be. I stayed with him because I had no options. I wanted you to have options. I rode your ass for a lifetime so you'd grow up to be independent."

"You broke me."

"No, I didn't. Look at you. Once your father was gone, you sprouted wings and flew."

Rage burned inside her. "I didn't sprout wings. You tossed me out. I had no choice."

"Exactly. Have you starved? Are you homeless? What's your life look like now?"

Riley considered her question. She wasn't homeless. She had a job. Money in her pocket. A man who loved her. She didn't need him, but she wanted him.

"You could have been nicer."

A sigh filled the void. "Yes, I could have been nicer. I could have been smarter. I could have been a lot of things. One thing I was, was honest. You were prettier once you lost the weight. While metal craft is a great hobby, it won't pay the bills. All I wanted was for you to be independent.

When I look at you and Baxter, I was a success as a mother."

There were a million litmus tests for success. Kathy's wasn't one Riley would have used, but she hadn't considered her objective. Hadn't considered Kathy's skill set or lack of one. Hell, Riley's own mother had bailed on twins shortly after they were born. All in all, she'd taken on a huge responsibility to secure her future. Maybe Kathy didn't need her resentment, but her gratitude, because in the end, she was proud of who she had become.

"I've never said this, but thank you."

Riley was certain the world stopped spinning, the birds ceased to sing, and the wind went still. The world was silent as Kathy wept.

"I've always loved you, Riley. I was never good at showing it."

She stared at the Bennetts' grave. It was evident Bea loved her family. It showed in the way her hand sat lovingly on her husband's shoulder and the look she had in her eyes as she stared at her daughter. There were lots of ways to love. Kathy's was tough. The lesson for Riley was she got to choose how she loved people, and she decided right then to love them completely.

"I love you too, Mom."

When she left the cemetery, Riley felt empty. Not in the way that left her destitute, but in the way that left her hungry for more.

She drove directly to Luke's. When she walked inside, she found him naked and waiting for her.

CHAPTER THIRTY

After a passion-filled night and a pancake-filled breakfast, they picked up her meager belongings and went back home.

Luke placed the last of Riley's clothes in his closet. "It's official, you're mine."

She wrapped her arms around his waist. "You're crazy."

"Crazy for you."

She pulled back and stared at him. "Would you have let me leave?"

"Yes, but I would have searched to the ends of the Earth to find you."

"I'm pretty fast, you know. It's all that clean eating."

"Baby, you may be fast, but I'll always catch you. A man can't live without his heart, and I've already given you mine."

"Are you seducing me, Mr. Mosier?" She ran her hands down her body to rest on her hips.

He looked at the bed and wondered if he had enough time to make love to her before the concert began. He took two stalking steps toward her before the doorbell rang and ended that thought.

Luke pulled her with him to the door.

In front of them stood Thomas, and in the back of his truck bed were the two sculptures she'd made for the concert.

"How? I saw them myself. They needed a power wash and minor repair."

Thomas smiled. "You're not the only welder in town. Turns out Bobby Williams had some equipment in his garage. He spent all week cleaning the pieces. Told me to tell you he's impressed with your skills. Despite the high heat of the fire, your welds stayed together."

Riley turned to Luke. "Did you know?"

"He set it all up," Thomas replied. "That damn love bug hit him like a hammer to the head."

Riley giggled. "I hear it's contagious."

Thomas held up his hand, giving her a five finger stop sign. "I'm inoculated."

"Someday, someone will worm their way into your heart."

He cuffed her chin. "I'm not an apple." He thumped his fist against his chest. "Heart of stone in a cell of steel."

Riley rose on her tiptoes and kissed Thomas's cheek. "Tell Samantha Luke will be late." As soon as the door closed, she pulled him into the bedroom and showed her appreciation.

That night at the concert, Luke set the fireworks alight

and watched Riley's eyes grow wide as her artwork sparked to life. Later, she took him back to bed and set his body on fire. "You're a damn firebug."

"Are we back to that again?" She laughed as she lowered her heat onto his length.

CHAPTER THIRTY-ONE

A MONTH LATER

Riley killed the flame to the welding gun and answered her phone.

"Hey Samantha, you back in town?"

"Yes. We did it. I can't believe we got away with it."

Sam had left with Dalton. Everyone thought they were going on a quiet getaway until Maisey let it slip they were heading to Vegas to finally tie the knot.

Everyone in town zipped their lips, which was quite a feat for Aspen Cove.

Maisey snuck away with Ben the night of the event to witness it with Sam's mother and brought back the photos of a drive-thru chapel wedding. They didn't dare stop for long, or they would have been mobbed by paparazzi and fans. They left Vegas and headed to Turks and Caicos, where they honeymooned the rest of the month.

"Do you feel different now you're married?" Riley always

wondered if somehow saying "I do" changed the way a woman felt about herself, her life, her future.

"Yes, I feel at peace. Dalton is a catch; glad to take him off the market."

"Once he met you, he was never on the market."

"Yeah, you're right. You know, when I met him, he thought I was an arsonist."

Riley laughed so hard, she had to hold her stomach. "What's with the men of this town and fire?"

"I have no idea. Anyway, I was hoping you could come to the Guild Creative Center."

"Let me clean up, and I'll be there in fifteen minutes."

Riley hung up and looked around the garage. She'd been working there since the fire.

The Lockharts were almost finished with the repairs, and she couldn't wait to get back inside her studio. Samantha's insurance had replaced her equipment, and she was itching to make something new. Maybe a fireman with a long hose?

She put everything away because she was a safety girl. Never again did she want anyone to accuse her of being an idiot or irresponsible.

She pulled into the parking lot and saw her brother's truck. With winter coming, the Lockharts doubled the crew on the Guild Creative Center and their new lake house. The projects provided an opening for her brother Baxter, who now lived above the bakery in her old apartment.

Samantha met her out front and handed her a check.

"What's this?" Riley looked down and saw $25,000.

"It isn't enough, but if you're willing to create more

instrument sculptures, I've got buyers." She explained how several of her friends, mostly musicians, wanted them for their homes and gardens, and now she was making a name for herself, she could charge more.

"This is twenty-five thousand dollars."

Luke pulled up and stepped out of his SUV with a bottle of champagne. "Congratulations."

Riley pointed. "You knew?"

He shrugged. "You know, it's a small town. Word travels fast."

While Riley knew Samantha was going to try to sell the sculptures, she couldn't believe she'd actually done it. She tried to hand the check back to her to help pay for the damages done, but Samantha refused. "I hear you've got good taste in tile. You'll need that." Sam turned around and walked away.

"You done for the day?" she asked Luke.

His head moved left to right slowly. "Nope. I've got lots to do." He raised the bottle of bubbly into the air. "I've got a toast to make, a girlfriend to propose to, and a bed to muss up."

She knew her smile was wide. Her cheeks ached from the strain. "Did you say you wanted to muss up the bed?"

"Is that all you heard?"

This time, her head moved back and forth. "No, I also heard something about a toast."

"You're killing me." He took a knee and set the bottle on the ground. From his pocket, he pulled out a blue velvet box. "Riley Black, you pulled into town, and I was an idiot. I should have listened to my heart the moment it told me you were the one."

She ran her hand through his hair. "When was that?"

"The second you put a quarter in the machine and played 'Ain't That a Shame.' That might have been the song playing on the jukebox, but in my head all I heard was, 'I Only Have Eyes for You.'"

He opened the box to show a simple solitaire. Not too big. Not too small. It was perfect.

"What do you say, baby? Will you be mine forever?"

She smiled. "Did you say we were going to muss up the sheets?"

"I did." He pulled the ring from the box. "And drink champagne. Is that a yes?"

She nodded. "Yes."

He stood and kissed her before he slid the ring all the way onto her finger. "You know what this means, right?"

She giggled. "Yes, it means I've taken Mr. February off the market."

"Let's go home and seal the deal with a toast and a tryst."

"Did you say tryst?"

"I couldn't say what I really want to do to you in public."

She leaned in and offered him her ear. "Then tell me."

He told her things that should make her blush, but all his naughty words did was make her run.

"Race you," she challenged as she hopped in her car and started the engine.

He called after her, "Baby, I told you a while ago, I'd always catch you."

Riley headed straight for home. It was hard to believe that only a few months ago, she'd pulled into town with little money and less hope.

She arrived with three things on her bucket list. To be an artist. To love herself. To build a life. She'd learned there were a hundred ways to live. A hundred ways to hate. A hundred ways to love. She came here expecting little but got so much from the town who took care of its own. In Aspen Cove, she found her family. She found her artistic passion. She found herself. She found the love of her life.

The past was in her rearview mirror, but so was her future. Luke was only a car length behind and closing the gap.

Next up is One Hundred Goodbyes

GET A FREE BOOK.

Go to www.authorkellycollins.com

ABOUT THE AUTHOR

International bestselling author of more than thirty novels, Kelly Collins writes with the intention of keeping the love alive. Always a romantic, she blends real-life events with her vivid imagination to create characters and stories that lovers of contemporary romance, new adult, and romantic suspense will return to again and again.

For More Information
www.authorkellycollins.com
kelly@authorkellycollins.com